BEST
LAID
PLANS

BEST LAID PLANS

A Colorado Black Diamonds Novel

EMILY SILVER

To all the Pipers of the world…stay soft, your Cash will come along <3

Prologue

PIPER

"That sounds like a great plan, sweetheart."

"Are you sure? It's not too lame?" I ask my mom on the phone.

"I know the team has been away, so I think Duncan would love spending some quality time with you."

"I've missed him."

The life of being a pro hockey player's girlfriend. My boyfriend and the Black Diamonds have been gone on a thirteen-day, six-game stretch. The team was dominant. You couldn't have asked for a better start to their season.

"I know when your dad played, I hated the away games. And that was only a few days."

"I just hope he likes this surprise."

"Trust me, he will." I can almost hear my mom's smile through the phone. "Tell Duncan we said hi."

"I will. Love you, Mom."

"Love you too."

I end the call and shoulder open the door of my small car. Grabbing the bag of groceries on the front seat, I head into the lobby of Duncan's building.

It's one of the more modern buildings in downtown Denver. The lobby is all glass and marble. Sunlight beams through the lobby in the early afternoon. It's way too fancy for my taste, with an ornate gold fountain in the middle of the outer courtyard, but Duncan likes it. Mainly because of the doorman. Because what professional athlete doesn't need security, he told me.

"Hi, Miss Fields."

"Hi, Ray." I wave to the older security guard who mans the front desk. "How was your family reunion?"

He gives me a big toothy smile. "It was wonderful. Happy to see all the grandkids come in from Texas."

"I'm glad you had a good time."

"Thanks for asking. I'll buzz you up."

"Thank you." I give him a smile before hoisting my purse higher up on my shoulder as I wait for the doors to open.

The elevator to the penthouse condo opens and I step in. The ride to the top of the building is swift. With each floor I pass, my nerves grow.

It's always like this after a stretch of away games. All I really get during these times is a few texts here and there. Duncan says he likes to stay in game mode and not break his concentration with phone and video calls.

I don't get it, but I don't want to mess with the mojo.

The elevator opens and I head to the one door on the top floor of the building. Windows look out over the bustling city. It's the perfect fall day in Denver.

Grabbing my key, I open the door to Duncan's place. It might not be one of the most exciting ways to welcome him home, but I love cooking. And it's one of the ways I love showering Duncan with attention.

Dating a hockey player is something I never thought

would happen. But when I started working for the Black Diamonds, I couldn't resist Duncan.

Those green eyes and that blond hair drew me in. I was a goner by the end of the first date.

Unlocking the door, I nearly trip over something in the entryway. Kicking it out of the way, my eyes are drawn to it.

A red lacy bra.

"What in the world?"

It's then a sound hits my ears. The deep moans of my boyfriend. And a second voice shouting his name.

Dropping the bag on the floor, I follow the noise.

I shouldn't. I know I shouldn't.

But what in the world is going on?

I take a deep, centering breath, trying to keep my emotions in check. Opening the door to his room, I'm greeted by his bare ass sticking up in the air. With a woman lying below him. Completely naked.

"What the fuck, Duncan?!" I shout.

"Shit." He flies up off the bed, dick sticking out between his legs. "What are you doing here, Piper?"

"Oh my God!" I recognize the female voice.

It takes me a second to place until she pops up to pull the sheet over her breasts.

"Ava?" My roommate. And supposed friend. "What in the hell are you two doing?"

"Better question is what are you doing here?"

"Me? You gave me a key!" My voice is bordering on shrieking.

"Not to use whenever you wanted." Duncan shifts a pillow over his steadily deflating cock.

"I thought you were going to be at the arena for a few more hours, and I wanted to surprise you."

"Piper…"

"Look, Piper—"

Ava and Duncan both talk over one another.

I hold up both my hands, not wanting to have this conversation with two naked people in a room that smells like sex and cheap cologne.

"Duncan, can I talk to you? In the living room?"

I leave the room. I don't think I'll ever be able to wipe that image out of my head. Of Duncan's bare ass sticking up in the air as he was fucking her.

My boyfriend and my roommate. How could I have been so stupid?

Stalking out, I'm a raging mess. When I talked to Duncan last night, he said he had practice today. Practice. How many times has he used that excuse and was instead fucking Ava? How many times had she blown off girls' nights to be with him?

Duncan struts into the living room in a pair of boxers. Ones that I gave him for his birthday. What an asshole.

For someone who just got caught cheating, he doesn't have an ounce of remorse on him. Not a single bit of regret. There's scratches down his chest and marks on his pecs.

"What in the world is going on, Duncan?"

"Babe, look…" He moves closer to me, but that's the last thing I want.

I wave my hands in front of him. "I mean, I know what was going on, but why?"

"Piper, babe."

"Stop calling me babe!" I scream. Duncan and his stupid nicknames. "You were fucking Ava! My friend!"

Duncan leans against the table, crossing his arms over his bare chest. His overly waxed chest. God, what did I ever see in this guy?

"I told you things weren't serious between us."

"You gave me a key," I tell him like it's the most obvious statement in the world. "Why else would you give me a key?"

"Piper, I can't be tied down."

"Can't be tied down? What does that even mean?"

Duncan scoffs. "Exactly what it sounds like. I'm not meant to be with one person."

"So instead of telling me like a grown-up, you decide to let me see you fucking my friend?"

Duncan at least looks a little remorseful at those words.

"Piper. It just wasn't meant to be."

I roll my eyes. "Thanks, Duncan. I'm so glad that you decided your dick couldn't stay in your pants and you had to go get action elsewhere."

"It was fun while it lasted, Piper, but I just don't see things working out between us."

"You know, I guess I should be thanking you. At least you saved me from wasting more time on this relationship."

Ava chooses this moment to walk out of his room. Her dark hair is still disheveled and she looks even less remorseful than Duncan. "Everything okay out here?"

"It's fine," Duncan tells her, wrapping an arm around her. She's wearing one of his shirts hanging down over her thighs.

How was I ever attracted to someone like him?

"You need to find somewhere else to live, Ava."

Bright side is it's only my name on the lease. She moved in with me when her place fell through at the last minute. Now I have an idea of what might have happened.

"I can stay with Duncan." She drags a black-tipped fingernail down his chest.

"Sure thing, babe." He drops a kiss on her lips.

"God, you two were made for each other. No class at all."

"Piper. Have some respect."

I roll my eyes, ready to slap the man standing in front of me. "Like the respect you're clearly giving me?"

"I think it's time for you to leave."

"Don't worry. The last thing I want is to be here a minute longer." I shake my head, walking to the door and grabbing my purse.

"Piper?" Duncan asks from behind me. I don't turn around, resting my hand on the door.

"What?" I'm seething.

"Things don't have to be awkward if we don't let them be."

"So what, now you want me to respect your decision and make it easy for you?"

"Easy for us both."

This time, I turn around, giving him the best fake smile I can muster. Digging his key out of my purse, I shove it at his chest. "Sure, Duncan. Easy for both of us. I'll make sure things are just peachy."

"Thanks."

He turns his attention back to Ava, missing the sarcasm dripping from my voice. I storm out of his place and head for the elevator.

This was not how I expected my night to go.

Dinner and maybe fooling around with Duncan, sure.

Walking in on him and my friend?

So much for surprising my boyfriend. I guess I was the one in for a surprise.

"How do you feel about today's loss, Cash? Does it sting?"

I blink. Blink again.

Who the fuck does this reporter think he is?

Of course losing to Dallas fucking stings. They're the worst team in the league, and we let what should have been an easy win slip through our fingers.

We lost. How does this guy think I'm supposed to be feeling? Ecstatic?

Fucking reporters. I hate these questions.

"Cash?"

"Well, it doesn't feel good."

"Do you think you getting into fights on the ice and giving Dallas two power play goals contributed to the loss?"

"Well," I start, "if the refs would have called the penalties against them since they were at fault, then maybe it wouldn't have made a difference."

It's not my fault the refs have their heads up their ass and can't see a penalty when it hits them in the face. The

Dallas guy hit me with a high stick first. I had to return it, didn't I?

"And how will you bounce back against Tampa?"

"Play better," I deadpan.

Seriously. What does he think I'm going to say? We're just going to lie down and take the loss and keep losing?

"And how do you plan on doing that?"

This guy is a good head shorter than I am. He has an air about him that he is a know-it-all of everything hockey. It makes me dislike him even more.

He probably did a quick Google search on what hockey is and then called it a day before getting this job. It shouldn't bother me as much as it does, but I can't help it.

Idiotic questions bring out the best in me like that.

He shoves the mic farther into my face.

Don't punch this guy, Cash. Stay calm.

"We're going to roll over and just give away the rest of the season."

"What?" He stares at me like I've grown a second head. I've thrown him off his game of asking each question he usually asks after the game. Not the PC answer he was expecting.

"What do you think we're going to do? It's one loss. It's not the end of the fucking world."

"I think that's all we have time for today." Cassie, our PR woman, appears at my side. "Thanks, Franklin."

He takes his dismissal better than I would have. The *Denver Tribune* reporter caught me in the tunnel before I made it to the locker room. Which makes me like him even less.

"Cassie—"

"Not now, Cash." Her heels click on the tunnel floor as I follow her back to the locker room. "Clean up and meet me outside when you're done."

Fuck me.

Just what I want after a hard game. A conversation with our PR manager. No doubt I'm going to get my ass handed to me for my responses in that interview.

From day one, we're given a strict lesson on how to deal with the press so we don't paint ourselves or the team in a bad light. Sometimes, it's just hard to handle after a tough loss.

As if it's not bad enough that we got beat on home ice tonight, but also answering inane questions from reporters? It's the last thing I want to deal with.

"Oh, sorry! Didn't see you there." A small body bumps into me. I look down at Noah Fields's little sister. A bright smile is pasted on her face and blonde hairs stick to her cheeks. "Sorry about the loss, Cash. You'll get 'em next time."

"You know we lost, right?"

"I know." She looks too chipper for the team losing. "You still have a winning record. One of the best in the league. I think you'll bounce back."

"You're about the only one."

"Cash! Don't keep me waiting!" Cassie barks at me before heading down the hall that leads to the corporate offices.

"Sorry. Guess you need to go."

"Yeah."

"Don't let them get you down." Piper gives my forearm a squeeze.

I don't respond, but watch as she heads toward the training room. There's a pep in her step that's hard to ignore. I shouldn't be ogling her. She's my teammate's little sister. But damn, does she have an ass on her.

When the door clicks shut, I shake off the ass-induced fog and head into the locker room. Instead of the jubilant, postgame celebration of a win, heads are hanging.

Some losses are harder than others. Losing to an opponent—one that we assumed would be an easy win—is always hard.

Walking around the Black Diamonds logo that covers the carpeted floor made to look like the ice rink in the arena, I head to my locker. From the day I walked into the arena, I was told it was bad luck to walk on the Black Diamonds logo. Maybe someone walked on it and that's the reason we lost.

I drop onto the padded leather bench seat in front of my locker.

Wooden lockers, lit up from above, line the room. The light has a blue tint to it for our team colors. Except tonight, it highlights the way everyone is feeling.

It smells like sweat and regret in here.

"Not the result any of us wanted tonight, men." Coach Barney isn't overly emotional. Only a big win or loss will get a reaction from him. Clearly that reporter needed to come talk to Coach B. If he's not worked up about one loss, why should the rest of us be?

"We'll take a look at the film tomorrow and see what mistakes we can clean up. Don't let this loss settle in. Brush it off. Tomorrow is a new day."

Maybe if I had said that to the reporter, I wouldn't have to go talk to Cassie. It's all adding to my mood taking a nosedive. I grab my towel and hit the showers.

Steam fills the shower room from guys already in here. I ignore all of them and find the last stall at the end. Where I always go after a game—win or lose.

I hate losses like this. Any loss sucks. You never want to be on the wrong end of a game when the final horn blows.

Especially when that voice comes back into my head.

The one that tells me I didn't play well and let my team down. How I'm a waste of space.

Fuck. This is why losses get to me even more some days.

Hot water sluices down my body, but it does little to help my shoulder muscles, tightly bunched around my ears.

I crack my neck and rinse off. No sense in standing here if it's not going to help my sour mood.

I sling a towel low around my hips and head back to the locker room. A few guys are already heading out, likely to meet their loved ones in the family suite.

I've never had anyone there to meet me. Not that it bothers me because I don't want my family here.

"Don't let it get you down, Cash." Troy slaps me on the shoulder as I dry off and slip back into my suit.

"Easy for you to say. I have to visit Cassie."

"Ouch." He winces. "What'd you do to incur her wrath?"

"Just being my usual delightful self."

"Don't know if I'd call you that." Troy laughs.

"Get out of here, cap. Go see the wife."

"See ya at practice tomorrow." Troy doesn't need to be told twice, running out to see his family.

Must be nice to have someone to go home to. Not that I don't love going home to my chocolate Lab, Puck, but it's not the same. Instead, I grab my wallet, keys, and Dopp Kit and head to Cassie's office.

The cinder blocks of the tunnel echo around my dress shoes. With the game ending so late, most of the staff hurried to get out of here and are gone.

Photos of bygone teams line the walls. The history of the team and its greatness presses in on you anytime you're here.

The Colorado Black Diamonds have been one of the

most successful teams in the history of the league. Even if we have an off year, we always bounce back. We are in the top ten of most Stanley Cup wins with four.

We pride ourselves on being the best. This is the only professional hockey team I've played for, and I want to keep it that way.

I pass through the glass doors of the executive offices and make a beeline for Cassie's. Her door is wide open since she's expecting me.

"Cassie." I drop down into one of the chairs in front of her desk. It's all glass with a black shelf behind her holding numerous degrees and awards.

A.k.a., don't mess with her.

"Can you not keep it together during a postgame interview?"

I guess she's not going to beat around the bush tonight.

"That reporter was a dick."

"And he was asking you the questions that any reporter would ask after a loss."

I roll my eyes. "And how many times do I have to answer that we'll play better next time? It's a stupid question."

Cassie opens her laptop and starts tapping away. "Do I need to go over the basics of PR with you again, Cash? You've known this since you were drafted. And don't even get me started on your language. Cash, you're supposed to be a role model for fans to look up to."

"I didn't ask for that."

"Well, it comes with the territory."

I grind my teeth together. I do know this, but sometimes, I'm tired. All I want to do is play hockey and not have to deal with the other shit that goes along with it.

"I know how to handle the press."

"Really? Because after witnessing you out there on the

ice and that disaster of an interview, I'm questioning whether you know how to do any of it."

"Cassie—"

"No." She cuts me off. "You should not have gone off on him. Weber is with the *Denver Tribune*, and they are one of our biggest sponsors."

"So I have to play nice so they don't pull their money?"

"No." She holds up a perfectly manicured finger. I'm surprised it's not her middle one—no doubt she's thinking it inside. "You have to play nice because you are starting to get a reputation. Your attitude on the ice—this pissy tit for tat—is going to get you kicked off the team. Penalizing someone because they did it to you first? This isn't kindergarten, Cash. And because of your performance tonight, on and off the ice, I'm going to have to spend my day tomorrow answering questions about why our top line player is turning into this jaded asshole."

"So ignore them."

Cassie gives me a pointed look. "Some of us actually have to do our jobs."

"What, like I didn't just play my ass off for the last sixty minutes?"

"Is that what you're calling it? I think you spent more time in the penalty box tonight than you actually did on the ice."

"Ouch."

"Look, Cash,"—she leans across the desk, and I know whatever is going to come next, I won't like—"you need an attitude adjustment."

"I do not," I grumble. "My attitude is fine. That reporter is fucking stupid."

"Yes, I really want this attitude to stick around," she says dryly, waving her hand around in front of me. "This isn't the first time you've had a run-in with the press."

"When were the others?" I ask, leaning back in the seat and kicking one Italian-loafered foot up on her desk.

Cassie wastes no time shoving it off and readjusting the picture of her wife and daughter on the table.

"Would you like me to start with *just* this season? Or would you like me to go back to when you were first drafted? Because you almost got into a fight with the reporter from *Sporting News Weekly*."

"Because he was being disrespectful to the women's team."

"Beside the point." Cassie holds up a hand. "You are a professional athlete, and your behavior reflects badly upon the Black Diamonds. And I'm the one that has to deal with it."

"So what do you suggest?"

Cassie casts an ominous look at me. Studying me. I shift under her hard stare. This is not a place I want to be right now.

"I need to think." She organizes a stack of papers on her desk. "But I can't do that with you here. Now go. I would like to go home to my wife and daughter before midnight."

She shoos me out of her office, ignoring the fact that she's the one that called me in here after a game on a Saturday night.

"Nice talking to you too," I tell her as I start to pull the door shut but am stopped when she says, "Be here bright and early on Monday morning. We'll talk more then."

"Looking forward to it."

"How are you feeling today, Nick?"

"Ready to get back to practice."

"Well, if you screw up your shoulder anymore, it's going to be hard to do that."

"It's not as stiff now," he tells me, rotating it like it's nothing.

I wave my hands to stop him. "I'll be the judge of that."

"I think I'm making good progress, am I not?" Nick hops up onto the exam table in front of me. He's wearing a tight, sleeveless Black Diamonds tank and athletic shorts. He's been more limited in practice since dislocating his shoulder during a game.

"You took a nasty hit, Nick. Let us do our thing."

"I'm antsy." As if to prove his point, he shifts on the table.

"Our backup is doing a good job."

"I still feel like it's my fault for every loss we take."

I roll my eyes as I grab the cuffs to start therapy with him. "Spoken like a true hockey player."

"Every shot that goes in is my fault."

Hockey players are so damn stubborn. I should be used to it since my older brother is also on the team—how I landed this internship—but the egos never cease to amaze me.

"You could say it's the defensemen's fault for not blocking them or blame the forwards for letting the puck get away from them."

Nick returns my eye roll with one of his own. "I get it."

"I could even go so far as to say it's the opposing team's goalie for blocking your shot."

"Ha ha." His voice is dripping with sarcasm.

"Now, are you ready to get started?"

The training room is quiet with practice not starting yet, and a few players in early to hit the ice. Nick hasn't been on the ice for a few weeks. With the way he landed on his shoulder blocking a hit against Chicago, it did more damage than expected.

"As ready as I'll ever be."

I attach the cuffs to his upper arms to help limit the blood flow to start the exercise. It's relatively new. Something that my professor in school taught us as part of a new study on restricting blood flow to help athletes heal and recover faster than with traditional therapies.

This is the first time I've been able to see it in action. I love being able to see something I've learned about working in real life.

My professor who was in on the study said it was revolutionary for athletes. And with a boss who is willing to try new methods, I got to take the lead with Nick's therapy under her guidance.

"Ten reps then take a break."

"I can do more."

"Ten reps only, Nick."

"Fine."

"Slow and steady. I don't want you overdoing it. If you want to hit the ice today for practice, take it easy."

"Really?" he asks, a hopeful look in his eye.

"As long as you don't overdo it, Claire said you're good to head back onto the ice."

I take a step back from him, watching his movements as he goes. It all looks good on my end. I love seeing that something I learned can help someone recover from an injury.

Especially a professional athlete.

Nick finishes his set, and I take the five-pound weights from him.

"How are you feeling?"

"Good. Does that mean I can get back out there?"

"You're lucky Claire said you could, because your sweet-talking wouldn't work on me. You forget, I've known you since we were babies."

Growing up, our dads were best friends. Having played for the Mountain Lions together, they all retired and stayed in Denver. Naturally, all of their kids became friends.

Nick is one of my closest friends since I'm only a few months older than he is. I'm lucky that I get to watch him play. He is easily one of the best goalies in the league, and the Black Diamonds know it.

Even though our backup is good, we've been feeling the loss of Nick with close games and easy goals that have slipped by.

"If only I was your type."

"No one you're seeing right now?" I ask, handing him the weights. A weird look washes over his usually stoic features.

"Not right now, no."

"You sure about that?"

"Drop it, Piper."

"Alright." I throw my hands up in defense. "Now, another set of ten then we're moving on to another exercise."

"Damn. You aren't taking it easy on me."

"Nope. You'll thank me for it when you're back on the ice."

"Will I?" he asks, laughing as he finishes his last rep.

The assistant coach walks in at that moment, eyeing everyone in the room. A few more players have drifted in since I started working on Nick. He casts a cursory glance over me and Nick before heading straight to my boss, Claire.

"What do you think that's about?" I ask, nodding at the two of them.

"Beats the hell out of me."

When he turns toward us with a grimace on his face, I know it can't be good.

"Are you the one in charge of Nick's rehab?"

I nod, crossing my arms over my chest.

"And what is it that you're doing with him?"

"What do you mean, what am I doing with him?"

There's an edge to his tone that I don't like.

"Coach Cooper, what are you accusing her of?" Claire asks. She's an older woman with graying hair who's been with the team longer than I've been alive. She knows what she's doing and wouldn't let just anyone help with rehab of the team.

Claire doesn't mess around, and I love that she takes chances on younger women in the field. Especially in athletics, where it's a male-dominated field.

"Does she know what she's doing with Nick here?" He waves a hand in front of Nick like I've asked him to dress as Santa Claus instead of doing a new, fully-vetted type of therapy to help his shoulder. "Is this so-called 'therapy' sanctioned by the team?"

The use of air quotes has ire burning through my veins. Typical of a man in a power position not thinking I know anything.

"I—"

"She wouldn't be here if she didn't," Claire comes to my defense. It prevents me from saying something I know I shouldn't. "It's a safe and effective exercise to help get Nick back onto the ice faster than traditional therapies."

"You're not going to take my goalie out for the rest of the season, are you?" He addresses my boss instead of me like I don't even exist.

I don't even know why I bother sometimes. People take one look at me with my blonde hair and think there's nothing in my head. That I'm a bimbo or a dumb blonde.

It's the furthest thing from the truth.

And I hate it.

"With this technique, he'll get on the ice faster than expected. Piper is working well with Nick to get him back where he needs to be."

"Under whose supervision?" He crosses his arms, like he doesn't believe either of us.

Claire bristles at his words. "Mine. We wouldn't be doing this if it would hurt the players."

"Coach, I'm fine," Nick pipes up from his spot on the bench. "Really."

"I'll stop by tomorrow to make sure things are still going well."

He disappears without another word.

"Don't let him get to you, Piper. You've been doing good work here."

"Sure." I nod at her as she goes to help out another

one of the players who took a vicious hit on the ice last night.

"Everything okay?" Nick asks when I make my way back to him.

"Fine," I bite out.

He continues through the slow movements of his exercise. Ones that have been vetted by everyone in the industry as cutting edge for athletes.

But it's supposedly me who doesn't know what she's doing. I've been studying and learning for years to do this. It hurts more than I'll ever let anyone around me know.

No one takes me seriously. They never have.

It stings more than it should when it's someone within the Black Diamonds organization that thinks that. I've more than proven myself to the team.

"You need me to keep going?" Nick asks.

"Let's take a break. Hit the treadmill for some cardio."

"Don't let them bother you," he tells me, hopping off the table with ease.

"I told you, I'm fine."

"I know you better than that, Piper. It was a dick move."

I laugh. "He's your assistant coach."

"Doesn't mean it's not true."

"I'm fine, really."

"Whatever you say."

He leaves me be as I go to straighten the pile of clean towels in the corner. I don't know why, but having something to do with my hands helps to soothe away the sting of emotions.

I hate that the coach's words bother me. It's not the first time I've heard them and it won't be the last. People have been underestimating me my entire life.

I'm more than just a pretty face. It's just…no one can see past it.

"Can I get a towel?" a deep voice rumbles from behind me.

"What?" I jump, my heart nearly leaping out of my chest. Cash is standing behind me, hands sitting on his hips.

Sweat has his shirt clinging to every muscle. It leaves very little to the imagination. Dark patterns of ink swirl on his arms. Black hair falls in front of his even blacker eyes. Light brown flecks flicker there.

Everything about Cash Williams is dark and closed off. Him talking to me startles me.

"You're muttering to yourself over here."

"I was not."

I actually have no clue if I was. It tends to happen when I'm mad.

"Sure." A slow smile plays on his lips. "Can I?"

He indicates to the pile of towels behind me. "Oh, sorry."

"Thanks."

I try to keep my eyes off him as he brushes past me. I feel his heat from his workout. He spends his morning in the training room with another trainer before hitting the ice.

Why I know his schedule, I don't know.

But it's hard not to notice Cash. The brooding looks pull me in. He's the complete opposite of Duncan.

After the way things ended with Duncan a few weeks ago, the last thing I need is to start another relationship.

With one of his teammates no less.

"Have a good practice. Don't overdo it."

God, could I sound any lamer? It's something I'd say to any one of the guys if they were in here, but saying it to

Cash? It makes me sound like the dumb blonde everyone thinks I am.

Cash doesn't respond or look at me as he leaves the room. I blow out a breath I didn't realize I was holding.

Why are nerves overtaking me at one hockey player looking at me?

He is not in my plans. I need to push past it. Ignore Cash Williams and the fluttery feelings in my stomach. It's not like he sees me anyway.

My focus needs to be on the other hockey players. The ones that don't distract me.

Not Cash Williams.

Because nothing good can come of having a crush on him.

Nothing good at all.

Chapter Three

CASH

"Cash, when you're done with practice today, can I see you in my office?"

Ugh, what now?

Cassie approaches from her end of the hall as I'm getting ready to hit the ice.

"I thought we didn't have to do this anymore."

"Oh, Cash, my dear. No, no, no." Her face has a maniacal twist to it. "You don't think so, but it needs to be done."

"Does it really?"

She holds up one perfectly tipped manicured finger before tapping on her phone.

"'Cash Williams—is he really worth the headache the team puts up with? by Franklin Weber.'"

For fuck's sake, I can't believe this is what I have to deal with.

Cassie continues, ignoring me, reading his latest article.

Cash Williams has been known as the perpetual bad boy. His behavior on and off the ice is something that no Black Diamond fan should have to put up with. Being the team bruiser, getting into fights on the ice, Williams's attitude and disrespect for the press is evident in every postgame interview. We never see him involved in any of the charities the team supports. How much longer will we have to put up with it?

"Cassie, come on, I don't have time to listen to this shit right now. I need to practice."

"We're all doing things we don't want to do right now. And I'd love it if you weren't a pain in my ass every day, Williams."

"Can I go practice now?"

She gives me that same twisted look on her face. "Fine, meet me in the office after practice. I have a plan to make all of this go away."

"Fan-fucking-tastic," I tell her through gritted teeth. I have a feeling whatever the plan is, I am not going to like it.

By the time I hit the ice, I'm fully distracted. Missing passes, easy shots on goal, and taking the ire of my team-mates around me.

"What crawled up your ass, Willy?" Duncan shouts my nickname from across the ice.

Tension is boiling inside of me, and Duncan the Douche would be a great outlet.

"Let it go," Troy says as he skates up to me, not letting me pass. "You're only going to make it worse."

"Why is he such a dick?" I grumble, skating back to the bench and taking a swig of water.

"Because he thinks he's God's gift to hockey."

"Just let me hit him once."

Troy laughs. "Sorry, Willy. Can't do that."

The whistle blows before Coach Barney tells us it's time for drills.

"Just the way I wanted to end practice."

"Dude, what's up with you today?" Troy asks. "You're usually not this distracted."

"It's Cassie, man. She read me that article by Weber today."

Troy waves me off. "We all know he just likes to start shit. I wouldn't think twice about it."

"Oh, so you don't think I shouldn't be a Black Diamond then?" I ask him, quirking a brow in his direction.

"Did he really say that?"

"He did, and I really don't want to have to deal with having to find another team."

"You should go play for the Knights, man. You'd probably fit in a lot better there," Duncan chirps, eavesdropping from his spot on the ice.

Fucking Duncan—he's the last person I want to be dealing with right now.

"And maybe you should go play for the Knights. You'd fit in a lot better there with your cocky-ass attitude."

"Enough chitchat, boys. Get to work." Coach Barney turns a steely-eyed gaze on us.

Apparently I'm on everyone's shit list today.

Duncan smirks back at me as we start the drills. Pushing my body this way is about the only thing that can clear my mind. It's hard to focus on anything else when your legs are on fire.

No matter how many times we do these wind sprints on the ice, it always hurts. But in the best way. Because building my strength now means we can go the distance as a team.

Hopefully straight to the playoffs this season.

The whistle blows to end practice as I skate past the line, nearly crashing into the boards. I'm gassed and need more than a minute after practice before I have to head to Cassie's office.

Hitting the showers, I let the water sluice over me as I take the time I need. Cassie is going to be pissed at me no matter what I do, so I might as well give my muscles a chance to relax.

I have no doubt by the time she's done with me, her mission is going to be to turn me into the team teddy bear. It's the last thing I want to be.

Teddy bears didn't get you anywhere when I was growing up.

Finishing my shower, I wrap a towel around my hips and head back into the locker room. Half the team is already gone, and I drop down into my stall, relishing in the relative quiet.

I know I can't put off the inevitable much longer. Steeling my spine, I slip into a pair of athletic shorts and a Black Diamonds T-shirt, then step into my gym shoes before heading down to her office.

The door is wide open. But Cassie isn't the first person I see.

No.

It's Piper.

What in the fuck is she doing here?

"Cash, please take a seat."

"What's going on?"

I don't take a seat as asked. My senses are on high alert. Why am I in here and why the hell is Piper here?

This can't be good.

Cassie's smile is sweet. Too sweet for my liking.

"Cash, as you know, we have a bit of a problem with your reputation."

"My reputation is fine," I grunt out.

"Do you really need me to read that article to you again? I can read more."

"No," I bite out, now dropping into the chair next to Piper.

Her blue eyes flit between Cassie and me, as if she doesn't quite know what to make of her presence here.

"What's going on?" Piper asks from her seat next to me. She's wearing her team polo and khaki pants. It does nothing for her. Not that I should be paying attention to her, but she's cute in a princess sort of way. It wouldn't surprise me if she had birds flying around her head. She's that sweet.

"Like I said, Cash, we have a bit of a publicity problem with you. And I, for one, don't want to keep having to deal with these articles about how you're not a team player and that you shouldn't be a Black Diamond. Do you want that?"

"No." This time there's a little less force behind my words. "I don't want that, Cassie. I like my spot on the team."

Actually, I love my spot on the team. The Black Diamonds have been my life since I was drafted. I don't want to have to change teams at this point in my career. I'm almost thirty. Who's going to want to pick up an aging hockey player at this point? Hockey players' careers aren't that long, and I'm definitely on the tail end of mine.

"Good. So, you are going to start dating Piper here."

"I'm sorry. What?"

"Is this what you called me in for today, Cassie?" Piper asks, leaning closer to her. She tucks a soft lock of blonde hair behind her ear. "You told me you wanted to meet to talk about something."

She waves her off. "Would you have come if I told you my idea? No, you wouldn't have."

Cassie is no-nonsense about everything. It's how she's gotten this far in her career, no doubt.

"Wait, so this is really your great idea? Cassie, you really think this whole…princess is going to help me change my image? She's Fields's little sister."

"Okay, I'm more than just his little sister, thank you very much." She glares at me from her chair. If looks could kill, she's trying really hard to put me six feet under. "And I'm not a princess."

I give her another once-over. Everything about her looks like a princess, even if she's wearing the blandest uniform the team has.

I ignore her. "Seriously, Cassie. This is the great plan to save my career? I don't think we could be more different if we tried."

"Exactly why I think she'd be perfect to help reform the bad boy of hockey."

"Are people really calling me the bad boy of hockey?" I quirk a brow at Cassie and lean back in my chair.

"Yes." One word. It's all she needs to make it stick.

Fuck.

Of course this is her solution. Make me look reformed by getting me a girlfriend.

"This is the only plan you have?" I ask.

"If your career didn't need saving to start with, we wouldn't be here right now. Now, the two of you"—she reaches into her folder on her desk and grabs two pieces of paper—"have a few team events that you need to go to in order to make this thing believable. I want you to have a few dates, go out to dinner, make Cash look like the loving boyfriend that he is so people don't start hating him. Maybe it'll even help your performance on the ice. And then I won't have to deal with you anymore."

"You know, you'll still have to deal with me because I'm on the team, right?"

"Hold on," Piper interjects. "I haven't agreed to this yet."

"I haven't either," I agree.

"You,"—Cassie points at me—"don't have a choice. Piper, on the other hand, you don't have to agree to anything. Take this home and think about it."

"Why me?" Piper asks.

"It makes the most sense. You work for the team and it'd be easy to pass off the two of you meeting while working."

"That makes me sound unprofessional. I've made it a point to never date players again."

"Again?" I shift in my seat to look at her.

"You don't know?"

"Know what?"

"I dated—"

"Look," Cassie cuts Piper off, "take the night to think about it and we'll meet back here tomorrow, okay? If you say yes, we can play it off as a fairy-tale romance."

"Because she works for the team? Not much of a fairy tale," I mutter.

"You wouldn't know a fairy tale if it slapped you in the face, Cash."

"Ouch."

Cassie goes back to ignoring me, something she's gotten very good at. "Think about it, okay, Piper?"

"Sure." Piper's face is more of a grimace.

Piper darts out of the office without a backward glance.

"Really, Cass?" I ask. "This is your grand idea."

"And what do you think we should do?"

I roll my eyes. "I don't know; why not a few team charity events?"

"The required events that are mandatory for you to attend? You can't just attend them. You need to make it believable."

"What if she says no?"

"She won't." Cassie has a victorious smile spreading across her face. "Your reputation is in the toilet, Cash. You bite off reporters' heads, people think you're unapproachable, and before you know it, you'll be cut from the team because of 'locker room problems.'"

I hate the way she uses air quotes.

Hockey has been my entire life for as long as I can remember. I'm not sure when the attitude came along. I mean, I know, but I'm not sure when I let it become my entire personality off the ice.

Being the ass is comfortable. Something familiar that I can depend on.

The wall that I can put up to keep everyone else out.

"How long would we have to do this for?"

"At least through the All-Star break."

"Jesus." I scrub a hand down my face. That's a few months from now. "You really think people will believe this?"

The difference between me and Piper could not be more night and day with her blonde hair, blue eyes, flawless pale skin.

Me on the other hand? A day's worth of stubble lines my jaw, and I have tattoos all up and down my forearms.

And a permanent scowl etched onto my face.

"People will believe anything they want to. You need to boost your image and can't do it on your own."

"Can I go now?"

"Don't cause any trouble." She dismisses me.

I head out into the office area, hoping to find Piper. I don't have to search far. She's pacing in front of the glass doors that lead to the exit from the offices.

"Hey!" I shout at her, grabbing her attention.

Piper's eyes snap to mine. "What, did she send you out here to convince me to go along with this plan?"

Grabbing her elbow, I steer her into a quiet corner. The ever-present ears in the office don't need to hear this conversation.

"Look, I wanted to tell you that you don't have to go along with this."

"I don't?"

Big, blue doe eyes stare up at me. Oh yeah, she definitely looks like a princess.

She's at least a full head shorter than I am. A tiny thing that I could fit into my pocket.

Not that I should be noticing that. That is the last thing I need to be thinking about.

I shake my head. "No. This isn't your problem. I can handle it."

Piper studies me. Her eyes take a slow perusal up and down my body. She's obvious in checking me out.

"Like what you see?"

Piper's eyes snap to mine. "Look, Cash, I can help you."

"I told you; you don't have to."

"What if there's something in it for me?"

"What would that be?" I cross my arms, leaning back against the wall.

"It would make Duncan crazy jealous."

"Why would you want to make Duncan jealous?"

"That player I dated?"

It hits me like a freight train. "You used to date the Douche?"

"You don't have to sound so astounded."

"I'm sorry, but now I'm beginning to question your judgment."

"God, you sound like my brother."

"I can't believe he let you date him."

"Excuse me." Piper raises her voice, punching me in the shoulder. I barely feel it. "My brother doesn't get a say in my dating life."

"Maybe he should," I mutter to myself.

"Excuse me." There's a fire lighting up her blue eyes now. "Noah doesn't *allow* me to do anything. He has no say over me and the choices I make. So if I want to do something stupid like agree to this little…proposal, if you will, then I can."

"I'm something stupid then?"

"Dating you? Yes, it might be the stupidest thing I've ever done."

"So does that mean you're in or out? Because you're giving me mixed signals."

"Do you want my help or not? Because it sounds like Cassie is ready to kick you to the curb, Cash."

"She doesn't have that power."

"If you're a nightmare for the team, how much longer do you think it'll be before you get traded? Really?"

Damn it. I hate that her words hold some truth. It won't be long before Coach Barney decides I'm not worth it and will have me traded to Nashville.

No one wants to go to Nashville.

"You really want to help me?"

Piper nods, a smile spreading across her face.

Fuck me. She's sweet. Almost too sweet to be doing this.

"Yes. I can help you and in return, it will help me stick it to Duncan."

"Because you want to get back together with him?"

She recoils from me. "Hell no. If there's one thing I can think of that would piss him off, it's me dating someone else."

"So you help me with my reputation and in return, we stick it to the Douche?"

"Why do you keep calling him that?" Piper asks.

"That's his nickname. Don't think it's fitting?" I take a step closer to her. She sucks in a breath, her eyes level with my chest and with the tattoos that cover my arms.

"I mean, yeah, I just haven't heard it."

"Even being in the locker room?"

Piper shakes her head. "I steer clear of the locker room. I'm only in the physio room."

"Good plan."

"So, are we going to do this?" Piper asks. "I'm in if you're in."

I weigh the pros and cons of this plan. If the two of us go into this with a clear goal of what we're getting out of this, it can't be that bad, right?

"We should probably discuss the finer points of how it will work."

Piper laughs, a sweet sound that hits me right in the gut. I ignore that feeling.

"How about we get together and talk it over then?"

I smile down at her. "Give me your phone."

I don't take my eyes off her as she pulls it out of her pocket and unlocks it.

Punching my number into her phone, I shoot myself a text so I have it saved.

"Okay, Princess, we're doing this."

Chapter Four

PIPER

Oh my God, am I really going to do this? That's the single thought that I keep focusing on as I sit at the bar waiting for Cash.

After exchanging numbers this afternoon, we decided to meet for a drink to discuss logistics. I know very little about Cash other than what Duncan has told me.

And based on the fact that Duncan told me, I don't know if I should believe it or not. The bad boy who sleeps with anything on two legs and gets into fights every other game? Cash doesn't seem the type, but what do I know?

The bar slowly fills up around me as I sit and wait for Cash. Glancing at my watch, I realize he's already fifteen minutes late. This does not bode well for the two of us to be doing this together.

Low music thrums through the bar. People come and go taking their seats at the hardwood bar top with the old rickety stools. TVs line the walls as do old beer posters. It's nothing fancy by any means, but I figured since it's a little more out of the way, people might not recognize Cash.

I have no idea if this thing is going to work. I don't

want people to see us together. Even if I say yes right now, we need to iron out the details.

Besides, don't we need to get to know each other before we start this thing? Because based on the little I know about him, it's not going to go well.

It's like my thoughts make him appear. He walks into the bar and he nearly takes my breath away. Jeans that cling to his strong thighs, a tight black tee, a leather jacket, and a baseball hat sitting backward on his head.

God, he really is too gorgeous for his own good.

I ignore the blaze of heat that fires through me and sit on my hands to avoid reaching out for him or waving like a moron. He already thinks I'm some little princess. I don't need to give him any more reason to think I'm an idiot.

I watch as his dark eyes skate over the bar before they finally land on me. I can feel his perusal from here, and it makes me squirm that much more in my seat. He takes long steps toward me, eating up the distance.

"Princess." He plops into the seat across from me.

I swallow down a sip of my drink. "What did I say about that?"

"Sorry. It's just hard when you look like you're straight out of a castle."

"No castles for me."

"You sure?" Cash eyes me, leaning back in his seat.

"Do you need something to drink? Is that going to make you less ornery?" I quirk a brow at him.

Cash ignores me, flagging down a server to order a beer.

A Breckenridge Avalanche.

"You think I'm ornery?"

"I can see why you get the bad attitude with the press," I mumble to myself.

"Are you always like this?" Cash asks as a beer is set in

front of him. He shrugs out of his jacket, exposing a long line of tattoos.

I can't help but drink my fill. Duncan was as clean-cut as they come. Manscaped to within an inch of his life.

Cash is the exact opposite. Sure, that's part of my reasoning for wanting to do this, but is it going to work?

"My attitude isn't the one that needs adjusting."

"It's not my fault reporters are dumb." Cash shakes his head at me.

"I'm not disagreeing that they ask stupid questions. You just can't tell them that."

"Did Cassie put you up to this?"

"You know I can think for myself, right?"

Cash shrugs. "Seems like something Cassie would put you up to."

I pick up my old fashioned and take a long sip, trying to cool the annoyance that is swirling inside me. All because of the man sitting across from me.

He needs my help. I don't want to *not* help him, but he's making it hard. I can see why Cash has such issues with the press.

His entire personality is *I don't give a fuck.*

Even the way he's sitting here in the bar—and that damn backward hat—says he doesn't care. His eyes are taking in the small bar. There's not much to it, but it's close to my studio and I like it.

"Is it that you don't care about the team?" I ask, studying him some more.

"What?"

"I'm trying to figure out why you're like this."

Cash snorts, swallowing down his beer. "Trust me, Princess. You won't."

"You have to give me something if we're going to make this work."

"What, you want to know why my childhood turned me into the fuckup everyone seems to think I am today? Hmm?" He quirks a brow at me, leaning across the table.

"It'd at least tell me something about you."

"No."

"Fine, then something else. Because right now, I don't see how this is going to work."

Cash shakes his head, finishing his beer. "Then we'll figure something else out."

"What, that's it?"

Cash nods. "Yup."

"You're right. I don't think this is a good idea."

"Fine," he bites out. "I don't need you."

"Good."

"Great."

I drop a twenty on the table and grab my purse. "Find another princess."

Cash Williams might just be the biggest dick on the planet.

That is a fact I'm sure of. And nothing can convince me otherwise.

Chapter Five

CASH

I was a dick. I know I was. But the more I thought about Cassie's plan, the more I hated it. How in the hell is dating someone going to change the fact that the press hates me?

It's nothing against Piper. I'm sure she's a nice girl—maybe with questionable taste given she dated Duncan.

Changing the weights, I start another set of reps. I need to work out the chaos in my brain before I hit the ice. It's an optional skate day. But with how I felt yesterday, I can't have another day like that.

My play hasn't been suffering. If it weren't for Puck, hockey would be all I have in life. It's the only thing I focus on. Is it a sad existence? Maybe.

Cassie might have a point, but I'm not going to tell her that.

I finish my set of reps, relishing the burn in my legs.

"Going to be a better day at practice?" Troy comes up to me, wiping his face off with a towel.

"I hope."

"You need to get out of your head."

"Believe me, I'm trying."

"Anything I can help with?" Troy grabs two water bottles and tosses me one.

"Do my postgame interviews for me?"

"Nah. They want to hear from our best defenseman."

"Don't let the other guys hear you say that."

Troy shakes his head. "Just have a few go-to things to say. Don't stray from that. Works for me."

"They love you and eat up anything you have to say. If you told them a question was dumb, they'd be apologizing to you."

"You've got this, Willy. Don't get in your head about it."

Troy leaves me be and I hit the treadmill for some cardio.

I'm only a few minutes into my warm-up run before I spot a familiar head of blonde hair.

Piper.

She's cleaning up towels and water bottles from the guys. Grunt work of an intern. I haven't had the balls to go tell Cassie that Piper is out. Mainly because she'll castrate me.

I crank the speed up on the treadmill and go faster. I need to push Piper out of my head, along with Cassie and this stupid plan to rehab my image.

It must work because by the time I'm looking up from the treadmill, Piper is gone.

I end the run and grab a towel before heading back to the locker room to suit up for the ice.

When I get to the hallway, the low drone of voices stops me short.

Piper is standing there talking to Duncan and some woman I don't know. I can't imagine how painful this must be for her.

All I know is she dated him. Based on everything I'm seeing, this is awkward. And that's before Piper moves to leave and ends up falling ass over heels and covers herself in sweaty towels.

I make up my mind.

I guess there's no going back now.

PIPER

THE DAY HAS GONE by without much activity.

With Nick back on the ice for practice, we don't see him as much in the training room as we had been.

He's working more with the assistant goalie coaches to get back into shape.

Because it's been a quiet day, I notice when Cash spots me while he's running, and I hate that I notice.

God, even just the look on his face gets me amped up.

Gets me riled up.

Cash wanted my help, but apparently he seems to think he can figure this thing out all on his own.

But that's fine. I don't need him. He doesn't need me.

I'm better off without him, right?

I can't imagine what Cash thinks when he looks at me. A spoiled, pretty little princess? A blonde bimbo? Someone who doesn't have two brain cells to rub together?

I don't know, but after last night, I don't know how anyone could ever pretend to be Cash's girlfriend.

I do my best to ignore him as I grab the empty towel bin and head to the equipment room and fill the bin with sweaty towels.

Grunt work, but it's what an intern has to do.

As I turn the corner, I bump into the wall and see two people kissing down the hall.

Of course, they're kissing in the hallway. Why can't I ever escape people and love?

Not that I have my own.

It's when they break apart that I notice who it is. Duncan and Ava.

I have no idea how Ava got here when the facility is closed to anybody but players and staff, but obviously, she somehow managed to find her way in.

I haven't seen Ava since she moved out the day after I found them having sex.

The last thing I want to do today is to deal with these two.

"Piper, it's so good to see you!" Ava exclaims.

"I can't say the same about you," I mumble to myself.

"Piper, why can't you be an adult about this?" Duncan chides me.

"You're right. I can be. I've got work to do."

"Laundry?" Ava asks, turning her nose up at me.

"Only helping out since the equipment guys are short-staffed." I give her the most charming smile I can muster before turning to leave.

Except making a quick exit does me no good when I run into the wall and go toppling over the wobbly cart.

Covering myself in dirty towels.

Oh my God. I've never really paid attention to how bad hockey players smell. I mean, sure, I have to deal with this on a fairly daily basis, but I've never realized how bad it actually could get.

Could this situation be any more embarrassing?

Lying on the floor covered in dirty towels, I wish a sink-hole would open up and swallow me whole. It'd be better than the embarrassment washing over me as Duncan and Ava laugh.

"Do you need help?" Ava asks. She couldn't be happier if she tried. I hate that my accident is causing her to be this elated.

As if she hasn't been gloating since stealing my boyfriend. Not that I care that much if that's how he was treating me.

I do my best to pop to my feet, dirty towels falling around me.

"God, you smell." Duncan twists his nose up.

"Because of you!"

These two make me feel like a child. Like they're humoring me by even talking to me. I wish they didn't make me feel so small.

But I do. Not that I'm helping myself in this situation.

"C'mon, Dunc, we better let the towel girl get back to it," Ava tells him, wrapping an arm around his shoulders.

Dunc? What a dumbass nickname.

"Not just the towel girl," I say. "Only helping out where they need me."

"No, she also has to touch everyone to help them get over their injuries." Duncan says this like I'm hitting on every player in the locker room.

Which is so far from the truth, I want to punch him. He's the one that hit on me. Told me how beautiful I was. How sexy. Never once complimenting me on anything else but how I looked.

I wish I could go back and smack some sense into myself.

"Ooh, maybe I should look at that job," Ava says.

"Sorry, Ava, I don't think that the team is hiring sluts right now."

"Piper, cut it out."

Even I knew that my comment was a bit below the belt. But when I'm around Duncan and Ava, I just can't seem to help myself.

After the way they treated me—my supposed boyfriend and friend, roommate even—I just can't help myself.

Between the two of them, they make me angrier than I've ever felt in my entire life.

"Hey, Piper!"

Oh God. As if this situation could get any worse, Cash is calling out to me. I turn, and he's coming directly at me. His face is unreadable.

"What are you doing here?" I ask.

"Princess, you said I was going to have to meet you out here when we're done."

Cash wraps an arm around my waist and hauls me close to him.

What in the world is going on? Is it a full moon and I don't realize it? Why is everyone acting so crazy today?

"Out here," I parrot back to him. Standing this close, I'm at least a head shorter than he is. Dark brown eyes gaze into mine.

"I thought we were going to grab lunch together."

"Lunch."

Cash drops a kiss on my forehead. I must have run into the wall harder than I thought because I don't have a clue as to what is going on right now.

"What in the fuck is going on here?" Duncan asks.

Well, at least both of us might get an answer to our question.

"Oh, Douche, I didn't see you standing there."

Cash pulls me in front of him, my back to his chest. I do my best to ignore how good it feels to be pulled tight against him. All those hard muscles against my back?

Definitely not focusing on how good they feel.

"What, sorry, you're the only one who's allowed to date around here?" Cash asks, dropping his chin onto the crown of my head.

"The fuck—are you two dating?" Duncan hisses.

"I'm sorry, what's it to you if I'm dating Cash?" I ask.

"I'm sorry, this man is not good enough for you, Piper."

"And if the standard of good enough for me is you, then everybody in the world would be better for me than you."

Duncan looks like he's trying to riddle that out, and it gives me more joy than necessary.

"Don't think about it too hard, Douche. You might lose what brain cells you have left."

Cash's words have me stifling a laugh. This was not how I saw this entire interaction playing out.

I guess Cash came to rescue his Princess.

"I'm serious, Piper. Does Noah know you're dating him?"

"You know, I'm really getting sick and tired of every single man in my life thinking they know better about what I need than I do."

Duncan glares down at me, crossing his arms. His biceps flex. He definitely wants to punch Cash.

"If you're making these kinds of decisions and dating Williams here, then you obviously need to have someone check your judgment."

Duncan's eyes are focused above me. Cash is taller than him. I can only imagine the look he's getting from Cash when Ava tugs on his arm.

"Come on, baby, we don't need to deal with these two."

Linking arms with Duncan, she drags him down the hallway. He glares at the two of us in their wake. I watch as they disappear around the corner before stepping out of Cash's arms and pushing him out of arms' reach.

"Okay, what in the hell is going on here? Am I in the twilight zone or something?" I hiss at him, in case someone walks by and hears us.

Cash shrugs. "You looked like you needed help."

"I was doing just fine."

"You were?" His mouth tilts up into a smile as he looks down at the pile of towels that I'm still standing in. "Because it seems to me like you're in a pretty smelly situation."

"Why'd you come to my rescue?" I ask. Whether I like it or not, Cash bailed me out of a situation that could have ended badly.

"Like I said, it looked like you needed help."

"But…" I let my words trail off as I think of last night and the moody man standing in front of me who wanted nothing to do with me. "I left you. I told you I wouldn't help you."

Cash scrubs a hand over his face. "Because I was a dick to you. The more I thought about this situation, the more it wasn't fair to you. I'm not the best at conveying my feelings to people."

"Really? Never would have guessed." I laugh.

"Oh good. There you two are." A new voice enters the hallway.

Cassie is the epitome of a power woman in her black pencil skirt and white blouse. The red soles of her shoes carry her directly to us.

"Piper. Have you given more thought to my *arrangement?*" Cassie quirks a brow at me before returning to the beeping on her phone.

"Listen, Cassie—"

I interrupt Cash. "I'm in."

It's a split-second decision, but Cash came to my rescue. As broody as he is, it's only right that I come to his.

What's a few months, right?

"You are?" they both ask at the same time.

"Why does that surprise you?" It steels my resolve. I want to prove these people wrong—that I can do this.

"I thought Cash would have scared you off," Cassie tells me.

"Hey!" he retorts.

"Fair." I laugh, not confirming to her that he almost did.

"I'll have a ticket at will call for you at tomorrow's game." Cassie is back typing on her phone. "You'll be with the rest of the wives and girlfriends, and I expect to see you in the family suite after."

"The family suite?"

"Have to make it believable." Cassie leaves in a whirl of expensive perfume.

Cash leans against the wall, crossing one ankle over the other. Sweat clings to him, his T-shirt sticking to his chest.

"Think you can make it believable enough, Cash?" I ask him. "We really need to sell this."

Pushing off the wall, Cash stalks toward me like a lion after his prey. My back bumps into the wall, eliciting a squeak. Cash loops an arm around my waist and I collide with his hard chest. I'm flush against him and all those muscles. Muscles I've only seen at a distance in the training room. I want to sink my fingers into the defined pecs. Lick them.

My hands grip Cash's shirt, holding him to me.

Cash's eyes darken as they stare down at me. His tongue darts out and licks his lips. His free hand cups my cheek, thumb running along my bottom lip. "You want me to pretend that I like you, Princess?"

Words and all common sense flee my head. I shouldn't be having a reaction to Cash.

"Yes." My voice is dry. Scratchy.

"Think this is believable enough?"

His eyes never leave mine. I want to look away, but I can't. Cash has locked me in his hold and I couldn't escape. Even if I wanted to.

I've never felt like this under another man's gaze. He's making me feel like we're the only two people in the world right now. That we're not in some back hallway in a hockey arena.

I tilt my head up, wanting more. More of this Cash, right now.

"Piper?" A shouted voice echoes down the hallway.

I shove Cash out of my arms, causing him to stumble over the empty laundry bin.

"Oh God! Are you okay?"

He catches himself against the wall.

"I'm fine," he says as he laughs. Those eyes of his have locked down again. Just when I thought the two of us were having a moment, it's gone.

Claire spots me as she turns the corner, seeing the mess I've made. "I need you in the physio room. Clean this up and then I need your help with some training."

"Got it."

Righting the bin, I start throwing towels into the empty basket before Cash's hand stills mine.

"Was that believable enough for you, Princess?"

"Yes," I squeak out. "Yes."

"We're doing this then?" Cash tips my chin up to meet his gaze. "I don't want to drag you into anything you're not comfortable with just because I helped you out."

"That's exactly why I'm doing this."

"Really?"

I nod. "You showed me a part of you that tells me you're a good guy."

"I'm not the good guy, Princess," he says, shaking his head.

"No?" I stand, throwing a towel into the bin.

"I'm the villain."

"I think you want to be, but really, you're Prince Charming."

"No one sees me that way."

I press a hand to his chest, getting close. Closer than I should. But if I'm now Cash's girlfriend—*fake* girlfriend—I can, right?

"Under all this ink and broodiness is a good guy, whether you want to believe it or not. I'll see you at the game tomorrow."

Chapter Six

PIPER

> Cash…

> Fine, Piper. As long as you don't hold up a sign that says "Hey Black Diamond Fans! Cash and Piper are dating to impress the media," you'll be fine.

> That'd be quite the sign

> Leave it at home <<winking emoji>>

> I'll be sure to do that

> Now, get that pretty ass of yours to the game

> Pretty ass, huh?

> It's a great ass

> You've noticed?

> Yes. But don't tell anyone

> Your secret is safe with me <<zipped lips emoji>>

> I'll see you after the game <<crown emoji>>

> <<eye roll emoji>> See if I wear your jersey now

I feel like an imposter.

Being in the WAGs suite with all the other family members? It feels like there is a neon sign above my head saying "FAKE GIRLFRIEND COMING THROUGH."

This thing isn't real, so couldn't I have sat in the stands with the other fans?

Taking a deep breath, I smooth out the front of my jersey—Cash's jersey—and head inside.

Gotta sell this thing, right?

The suite is massive. Pictures line the wall from the team's Stanley Cup victory a few years ago. A well-stocked bar sits directly to my right and platters of food are laid out to my left. A small grouping of chairs sits in front of TVs that show the players warming up. And just beyond them is the glassed-in area with our seats for the game.

Only a few people are here, but I notice Angie right away. She's hard to miss.

"Piper. What are you doing here?"

The second her eyes lock on to mine, she looks confused.

I guess now is as good of a time as any to rip the Band-Aid off.

"I'm here for the game." I try to inflect some levity into my voice that I don't feel. Maybe it will stop the torrent of questions that I know will come.

"I know that, but…" Her brown eyes glance down, noticing my jersey. "Whose jersey is that?"

"Cash's."

"Cash? Are you with Cash?"

I nod, shoving my hands into my jean jacket pockets. Otherwise, I'll turn into a fidgeting mess.

"Wait, like dating him?" Angie pulls me to the side.

"Like dating him," I confirm.

She's wearing her husband, Troy's jersey. Number twenty-two with a newly emblazoned captain's logo.

"Since when?"

Angie sounds as confused as I feel.

"A few weeks," I blurt out.

I really should have thought more about this before I

got here. If anyone had asked, it was easy enough to tell them how we met.

Like Cassie said—a fairy tale of two people falling in love at work.

"How did I not know this?"

I shrug a shoulder. "We've been keeping it under wraps."

"I'll say." She nods behind her. "Want a drink?"

"Sure."

"We had the team cookout a few weeks ago and I didn't see you there." Angie casts a wandering eye at me as I order an old fashioned from the bartender. It's about the only thing I like and will help calm my nerves.

"Oh, that." I stall, sipping on the sweet and smoky drink, a favorite of mine that I picked up from my dad. "I had class."

That seems to satisfy her. "I don't miss those days."

"You're telling me. I'll be done with my master's in the spring and then get the fun task of job hunting."

"What are you doing now?" Angie takes her glass of white wine and points toward the seats.

"I'm finishing school for PT, and doing an internship with the team."

I follow Angie to our seats. "How's that going?"

The arena is starting to fill as it gets closer to the puck dropping. Both teams are out on the ice warming up. My eyes immediately lock on to Cash.

It's hard to miss him down there. He has a presence on the ice that is unmatched. The way he skates is powerful. Like the blades of his skates are an extension of him.

I don't think I ever noticed Duncan like this. And we dated for a few months.

God, I really need to get it together.

"Piper?" Angie nudges my shoulder. I completely missed her question.

"Hmm?" I turn my focus to her. "What were you saying?"

"The feeling doesn't get old."

"What feeling?" Now I really have no idea what she's talking about.

"Watching your guy out there on the ice."

"He's—" I'm about to say he's not my guy, but stop myself. "He's really good."

"Really good?" Angie practically has to pick her jaw up off the floor. "He's one of the best players on the team."

I sit forward, resting my elbows on my legging-clad knees. I can't tell much from a warm-up, but I know Cash is good. His reputation precedes him, even if it might not be for the best reasons.

"I don't want to sound cocky."

Angie laughs. "All hockey players are. You can brag about Cash if you want. I won't say anything."

The seats start to fill up around us. I don't recognize half these women, but I know their significant others based on the numbers they are wearing. Some are wearing bedazzled jerseys and dressed to the nines, but others, like Angie and me, are in simple pants and our jersey.

The teams leave the ice as the pregame starts. Fans start cheering as the lights go down. Bright spotlights start to flash through the rink.

A video of the players, all of them looking like badasses, starts to play on the jumbo screens hanging over the ice.

Energy thrums through the arena like a real-life, breathing thing. It's palpable.

From what I can see, not a single person around us is

sitting down. Boos echo as the opposing team skates out onto the ice.

The orange and black of Vancouver's jerseys are a blur as they skate around their end of the ice. People are banging on the glass. It's electric.

Then, the lights shut off completely. The music changes to a low bass, steadily increasing before the Black Diamonds are announced. The fans go wild. Angie and I cheer right along with them as the team skates onto the ice. Cash skates out, followed closely by Troy, and Angie loses her mind.

Butterflies are swarming inside me as I track him across the ice. Both teams are out there now as the Black Diamonds announce their starting lineup.

When Cash's name echoes throughout the arena, a burst of something explodes in my chest.

Pride.

Cash and I have been at this thing for, what, twenty-four hours? And all I feel for him is pride.

I don't know what it is about his reputation that Cassie isn't on board with. From what I can see, the fans are eating this up. Not that anyone would boo one of their own during a game.

After the national anthems of both the US and Canada are played, the game starts. There's no denying that Vancouver is a good team. Great, even.

But they are no match for the Black Diamonds.

The team is fluid, moving as one across the ice. The play sets up, with our team easily driving the puck toward their goal.

Troy. Cash. Noah. Back to Cash. Before he sends it up the ice to a winger who scoops it up and sends it flying into the back of the net.

"Yes!"

The red light flares as the horn echoes out across the arena. I'm jumping up and down right alongside Angie, celebrating the first score of the game.

They make it look easy.

"What's going on?" I ask. Stuffed animals of all kinds are being thrown onto the ice.

"Every time they score tonight, fans throw stuffed animals onto the ice. They'll take them to the local children's hospital later this week."

"I love that." Play temporarily pauses as members of the team skate onto the ice to collect everything. "I can't believe how many are out there."

There have to be hundreds lying on the ice.

"It's because we have the best fans," Angie tells me.

"You don't have to sell me on being a fan."

The minute my brother got into hockey when he was younger, the entire family became fans of Colorado's NHL team.

I've known of Cash since Noah was drafted. He's not an easy person to get to know, but since we started this thing, I'm determined to get to know him. At least as much as he'll let me learn about him.

The game picks up again, and I take the opportunity to refill my drink and grab some pretzels with cheese.

"Are you going to go with Cash to hand them out?" Angie asks, stealing a pretzel off my plate as I take my seat next to her.

"Am I allowed to?" I drag a warm pretzel through the beer cheese and take a bite. "I thought those were players only."

I don't know if it was on Cassie's official list of events, but I didn't look too hard after I left Cash the other night. I guess I should look more closely.

"I think it'd be a great idea. Let people see a different side of Cash."

A smile erupts on my face. "I can't imagine how cute he'd be with kids."

Under all the broodiness, I feel like there has to be a heart of gold. Maybe there isn't; I don't know. I'm hoping with time Cash will show me his true self.

Sure, he stepped up for me with Ava and Duncan, but that could've been a one-off. I know very little about my boyfriend.

My *fake* boyfriend.

A fight breaks out on the ice, distracting the two of us. One of Vancouver's players has his gloves off, going at it with Duncan.

I lean over, whispering to Angie, "Is it bad I hope the Vancouver guy punches him in the face?"

Angie peers around the suite, most people lost in their own conversation. "Just don't let the others hear you."

Duncan gets sent to the sin bin and I groan on behalf of the team. Playing a man down is never easy. If only the Vancouver guy had gotten a piece of him.

Cash is on the ice, working hard to defend our goal and kill the power play. Fans are on their feet cheering loud as Vancouver is circling.

A bad pass from Vancouver has Cash grabbing the puck and streaking down the ice.

Cash's stick-handling skills are doing something to my insides that Duncan never did. It's intoxicating watching him, the way he dodges between the defenders and breaks away toward Vancouver's goal.

"Go! Go!" I'm out of my seat, jumping up and down, cheering him on. He cranks the puck toward the goalie, and it sails just over the tip of his glove and into the net.

The horn sounds as the stands erupt.

"Yes! Way to go, Cash!"

I know he can't hear me, but I'm bursting as I watch the team crowd around him to congratulate him on his goal. More stuffed animals rain down onto the ice.

"I don't think I've ever seen such an incredible goal. On their power play no less!"

Angie wraps an arm around me, pulling me into a side-arm hug as the game resumes. "It's a high, right? I love watching Troy out there. He's so good, it's mesmerizing to watch him play."

"That's it exactly."

I sip on my drink, trying to cool my cheeks. Cash is now on the bench as Vancouver is trying to tie it up before the end of the first period.

I could get used to this. Watching Cash play and hanging out with Angie? I thought I would be more nervous, but she wiped out any nerves that I had about being here tonight.

Nick easily blocks another shot on goal before Colorado is taking it back down the ice. It's easy to see how skilled they are.

"Is it weird your brother and husband play on the same team?" I ask Angie.

She laughs. "I don't think I ever thought Nick would get drafted by Colorado, but I guess they want to keep the Colorado kids in Colorado."

"Helps that he's one of the best goaltenders in the league."

"And yet, he's still my annoying little brother."

"I guess it's the same with Noah. None of them went all that far."

"Maybe because they're some of the best players in the league and Colorado was smart to pick them up."

The horn sounds for the first intermission as the team

leaves to the cheers of the crowd. Colorado is up 2-0 early in the game. If things continue like this, it's going to be a good game.

And that's exactly what happens.

Colorado dominates Vancouver with a final score of 5-2.

"Do you always feel like this after a win?"

My voice is hoarse and scratchy as Angie links arms with me and leads me to where we'll meet the guys.

I'm anxious to see Cash.

A few families are already there. Little kids are running around the carpeted room decorated with squishy sofas. It's nothing fancy, but comfortable. A few of the guys are already coming in after the game. I bet they didn't have to talk to the media—something Cash probably wishes would happen to him.

But after that goal he stole on Vancouver's power play, they'll be eating up what he has to say.

Before too long, he's walking into the suite. Cash has a presence, all eyes seeming to turn to him as he walks toward me.

His stride is powerful as he closes the distance between us.

"Cash."

"Princess."

"I'll give you that since you had such a great game tonight."

"Yeah?" he asks sheepishly.

"How many teams score when the *other team* has a power play? Not many."

"It felt really good."

"It was great, Cash."

Cash rubs a nervous hand on his neck. "Listen, I know

you're working tomorrow, but want to come to the hospital with me? To hand out stuffed animals."

"Sure."

I know he's only asking me because we have to look like a couple. But I like that he asked me without saying the reason why.

"Great. I'll text you my address. Maybe you can meet me there and we can go together?"

"That sounds great."

"Great. Sounds like a plan."

Great.

Chapter Seven

"Are you going to be a good boy for me?" I'm sitting on the floor, playing with Puck. Piper is supposed to be here in a few minutes.

It seems weird that she's coming with me to the hospital, but who am I to argue with Cassie?

The doorbell rings and Puck goes running toward his bed.

"It's okay, bud. I promise."

Puck doesn't like people. I adopted him from a local Lab rescue when he was a few months old. It took him a while to warm up to me, but now? I'm one of the only people he likes.

Swinging open the front door, I'm met by the sight of Piper, standing there looking way too gorgeous for her own good. Tight jeans. Black, silky top and a simple jacket. Her blonde hair hangs loosely around her shoulders. Her makeup isn't overly done.

It makes her even sexier.

Which I have no right to be thinking.

"Princess."

"Cash." She brushes by me as I wave her in. "Nice place you have here."

"Thanks. It's not much."

"Better than my brother's place. If it weren't for my mom, he'd have a card table for a kitchen table."

My house isn't big. It was hard to fight the idea that my entire hockey career could be taken from me in one hit.

It didn't mean that I didn't want a warm place to come home to. The first thing I did was hire a designer to make it a place where I wanted to spend time.

Dark, hardwood floors cover the entire first floor. Brown leather sofas fill the living room, facing a brick fireplace where a TV hangs. All the walls are a dark blue. I thought it would be too much, but I like it.

Various trophies I've gotten through the years sit on the shelves that line the walls from the living room to the kitchen. The puck from my first score in an NHL game. Small things that I wanted to keep instead of pictures of family.

"Who's this?" Piper asks, walking into the living room.

Puck's tail, where it's normally tucked between his legs when he meets new people, is wagging.

"My dog, Puck."

"Puck? That's adorable."

"I wanted to name him Gretzky, but the day I brought him home, he went straight for one of my pucks and wouldn't stop chewing on it."

"Then I guess it's a good thing he got a puck and not something like toilet paper," Piper laughs.

God, she's cute.

"Careful. He's not big on people."

"Hi, sweet boy." Piper squats close to him, holding her hand out so he can sniff her. Big brown eyes look at her hand before he leans toward her. A few sniffs and he's up and attacking her face with kisses.

Piper falls on her ass as he licks every inch of her he can get to.

"Easy, boy."

Of course my dog likes her. I've never seen him take to anyone like that. Not even me.

"What a good boy. Yes, you are," Piper coos. Puck drops into her lap and leans into her pats.

"He likes you."

"Makes one person in this house."

"Aren't you funny."

Piper gives him a pat on the stomach before pointing him back to his bed. "Your dad and I are going out today, but I'll have him home in one piece."

Puck lies down like he understands her.

"We better get going."

I don't need my dog to fall in love with her any more than he already has.

"Are you nervous about going to the hospital?" Piper asks as I lead her into the garage to head out.

"Not really." I open the door to my truck and help her in. "Kids don't criticize nearly as much as adults."

Piper's laughter follows me around as I get in and head toward the hospital. "So the way to befriend you is to not criticize?"

"Well,"—I turn my blinker on and merge onto the main road through the city— "would you want to be friends with someone that criticizes you?"

"I kicked that person out. Not that she was critical, but just a terrible person."

"Who did you kick out?" I can't imagine anyone being a terrible person to Piper.

"Ava."

"Wait. Ava was your roommate?"

"Mm-hmm."

"Jesus, Piper."

"I'm glad to be done with those two."

"Even if we keep running into them?"

Piper groans, covering her face with her hands. "Could that have been any more embarrassing?"

"I don't know." I come to a stop at a light. "You looked pretty cute covered in towels."

She fixes her eyes to me. "You do realize how bad those smelled, right? I blame you."

"What? Because I used a towel that day?"

"Hockey players in general. Sweat less, will you?" Piper laughs.

Even though her roommate and boyfriend screwed her over, there isn't much bitterness that I can detect in Piper.

"Sorry, Princess. I don't know if that will happen."

"Damn."

"How'd you get the job with the team anyway?"

It's easy conversation. The least I can ask since she's doing this with me.

"I'm getting my master's in physical therapy. Noah helped me get the job."

"Wow. I'm impressed."

"You are?"

I nod as I pull into the hospital parking lot. "I couldn't do that much school. I was never the best student."

Piper nods, getting out of the car. "I enjoy it. Learning new techniques to help athletes heal? It's fascinating."

Placing a hand on Piper's back, I guide her into the hospital. A few of the guys from the team are already there, along with a few reporters.

"Cash. So happy you could make it today." Cassie

beams at me. "All of the kids are gathered in one of the main rooms, so we'll be starting there."

"Sounds great."

"I'll hang back and let you do your thing, Cash." Piper gives me a grin as I follow Cassie to where we need to be.

The hospital walls are painted a basic beige with photos of Denver adding the only color. I wouldn't want to spend any time in here.

The second we cross into the children's area, the walls change from beige to a bright blue. Clouds are painted with birds and the sun covering them.

Nurses in colorful scrubs are waiting for us. "You must be Cassie. I'm Lindsey, the charge nurse. We're all so excited to see you."

"Thanks for having us."

"We're in the reading room. It's all the kids can talk about today."

A tug comes on my sleeve. I have no idea how old this kid is, but his arm is in a sling and glasses sit on his face. Blond hair falls over his forehead.

"You're Cash Williams." He shoves his glasses higher up on his face.

I squat down to his level. "I am. What's your name?"

"Mikey."

"Mikey. What'd you do here?" I ask, pointing to his arm.

"I broke it playing soccer."

"Is soccer your favorite sport?"

He shrugs the shoulder that isn't in a sling. "I like all sports. It's my favorite to play. Mommy won't let me play hockey until I'm bigger."

"Well, maybe you should listen to your mom," I tell him.

"She said when I get better, she'll take me to a game."

I turn to Cassie and she is already waiting with what I need. A bright green stuffed turtle.

"Well, maybe this will keep you company until you can come to the game."

Mikey takes the turtle from me with a happy look on his face. "Can you sign my cast? Please?"

"Sure thing."

I turn around, asking for a marker, and Piper hands one over. Her phone is in the other hand, snapping pictures.

I know she's doing this so we can post about our relationship on social media. But her doing it instead of the reporters feels different.

Almost like she's proud of me. I scrawl my signature on Mikey's cast and take a picture with him.

"Thanks, Cash!"

"Anytime, Mikey."

"C'mon, let's go back so you can meet the rest of the players," the nurse calls to him.

The rest of the afternoon is just like this. Little kids chattering my ear off. Hearing all about favorite sports, TV shows, and annoying siblings. Passing out the stuffed animals that our fans brought to the game.

All of the guys are loving this. It's hard not to when the kids are so joyful, even though they're in the hospital.

Piper gets in on it, answering questions the kids ask her and handing out stuffed animals to any kid that's there.

By the time the day ends, instead of being exhausted, I'm on a high.

"Who knew you were so good with kids?" Cassie sidles up to me as we leave the hospital. "Everyone was telling me how great you did in there."

I shrug a shoulder, brushing off her praise. "Kids are easy. They don't yell at you when you mess up."

"Sorry, Cash. That's my job." Cassie pats me on the shoulder. "Enjoy your night."

"You too."

Piper is waiting outside for me in the cool evening.

"You were great today," Piper tells me as I walk up to her.

It means more to me coming from her. "I told you; kids are easy for me."

Piper is beaming at me. "Cash, they loved you. It was incredible to see."

I look around. The city is bustling around us as people are coming and going at the early evening hour.

Something about this day makes me not want it to end. Whether it's from having a good day, spending time with the kids, or Piper, it has the next words spilling from me before I can stop them.

"Want to grab a drink?"

"Yes," she answers with no hesitation.

"Good."

Because spending the night with Piper is how I want to finish this day.

"Where in the world are you taking me?" Piper asks, grabbing my hand and stepping in close.

"Some place where we don't have to be on."

A cowboy sitting on a horse is painted on the side of the old building. I grab the door of the Moon Bar and hold it open for her.

"This place okay?" I ask as she floats by in a cloud of sugar. I don't know how she smells so sweet, but she does. Like a cupcake I want to sink my teeth into.

For a weeknight, it's quiet. After being photographed to within an inch of my life today, I wanted to go somewhere I could be myself. Where people wouldn't bother me for an autograph. I love getting to do events like we did today, but I need to decompress now.

Christmas lights hang from the acoustic ceiling tiles. A few people linger around the bar, and someone is on stage getting ready for karaoke.

"It's great, Cash." She spins on her heel, giving me a smile before finding an open table in the bar.

"What do you want to drink?" I ask her.

"Old fashioned."

"Really?"

Piper slides into a chair. "What, think I can't handle it?"

"No."

Piper leans across the table. "I can handle you, can't I?"

Damn. "Okay then. One old fashioned coming right up."

I wink at her before heading to the bar and getting her drink and a beer for me. With practice tomorrow morning, I need to be on my game. A long road trip is coming up and I don't want to be gassed before we start.

"Usual, Cash?" the older bartender asks me.

"And an old fashioned with top-shelf bourbon."

"You got it."

Grabbing my wallet, I tap my card on the bar waiting for our drinks. The TV is playing the Nashville game.

"Seriously, Roy? You have this shit on?"

He scoffs at me, mixing Piper's drink. "Guys want to watch it. Sue me."

"Need to think twice about who you let in here."

"I let you in, don't I?" He sets the two drinks down with a toothy smile.

"See if I come back."

"Fuck off."

There's no malice in his words. Roy has owned this joint for as long as I can remember. He's why I keep coming back. I let him swipe my card, and I pull out a generous tip for him before heading back to our table.

And what I see has me stopping in my tracks.

Piper slips out of her jacket, dropping it onto the back of her chair. My mouth is dry as I stare at her bare back. The black, stretchy material clings to her. Lace lines her shoulders, showing a diamond cutout on her back.

Pale, perfect skin.

I want to lean over and kiss each notch of her spine.

She's been wearing this all day and I haven't noticed?

I set the drinks down on the table and take the seat across from her.

Fuck. I shift on the seat, trying to control the growing problem in my pants.

"You okay?" Piper asks.

"You have no idea."

Her smile is soft. Hell, everything about her is. Piper has half her hair pulled back into a fancy twist, bun thing and is wearing a light layer of makeup.

Soft.

Sweet.

Like a fucking princess.

Piper grabs her drink and takes a small sip. "Mmm. Thanks, Cash."

"I never would have pegged you for an old fashioned drinker. You seem awfully young to like bourbon."

Piper sets her drink down and leans across the table. She grabs a pretzel from the bowl that sits between us. "When I turned twenty-one, my dad gave me my first drink of it."

"And let me guess, you loved it," I interrupt.

"God no." She laughs. "I hated it."

"Really?" I take a long pull of my microbrew.

"It took me awhile before I liked it. I like the simple syrup and cherries in it."

Piper fishes in her drink for the cherry and pulls it out by the stem, grabbing the sweet fruit between her teeth and biting it off.

Fuck. Me.

I take a healthy swallow of my beer, trying to cool the heat that's flowing through me, straight to my groin.

Piper licks her fingers, dropping the cherry stem on the cocktail napkin.

This woman is driving me fucking crazy. She makes it hard to be around her, but makes me want to be around her more.

It's dangerous. Because Piper isn't mine. This thing is fake. But it doesn't mean I can't pretend she's mine for a little while.

"Okay, so I know nothing about you, Cash. Tell me some things."

"Like what?"

"I can search you online and find your college stats and how many goals you scored with the Black Diamonds when you won the cup a few years ago. But that's it."

"If that's all you found, then that's a good thing."

"Why?"

I snort around my drink. "Because it's usually not all that good."

Piper gets a cocky look on her face. It shouldn't be as cute as it is, but I like it. "Then why don't you tell me about you?"

I take a hearty sip of my beer. "I walked right into that, didn't I?"

"You did." Piper bites into one of the pretzels. "Now, favorite color?"

"Out of all the questions in the world, that's what you're asking me?"

"You can tell a lot about a person by their favorite color."

"If I tell you mine's black, what does that tell you?"

Piper leans across the table. This close, I can see small flecks of green in her blue eyes. "You're lying."

I lean closer. We're less than a foot apart. I can read Piper like a book. I don't know how she can tell I'm lying, but I am.

"Fine. It's red."

"I see." She leans back in her chair, sipping on her drink.

"Gathered all you needed to know about me with that one fact?"

"Red means you're passionate. Ambitious. Need a sense of adventure. Like sex."

"I'm a man, Piper. Of course I like sex."

Which now has me thinking of sex. With her. And that damn top that clings to her that is driving me wild. So much for not thinking about her like that.

"Tell me something I don't know." She rolls her eyes.

"Okay, fine. How do you know so much about color meanings?" The less I think about sex, the better.

"I like learning about these things. You can tell a lot about a person by their favorite things."

"What's yours?"

"Purple."

"What does that say about you?" I ask.

"We feel deeply. Are compassionate. A good judge of character."

Hooking my leg around the leg of her chair, I pull her closer toward me. Her eyes widen in shock. Piper's tongue darts out of her mouth and wets her lip.

What she's feeling is written all over her face. I don't want to notice, but I can't help it. I'm finding I notice everything about Piper.

"What does that good judge of character tell you about me?" My voice is low, husky. It doesn't hide the way she's affecting me.

A finger traces the tattoos on my forearm that rests

between us. Piper looks at my arm and then up at me before repeating the motion.

It's lust-inducing. Making me chub up in my jeans.

There goes any chance of not thinking about Piper.

Naked.

Under me.

Watching her take my cock.

Fuck, would she ever look good with me inside of her.

"You do everything you can to keep people out, including tattooing a brick wall on your forearm."

I gaze down to where she's tracing the ink that wraps around my arm. It was one of the first tattoos I got when I turned eighteen. Out on my own with a chip on my shoulder, I wanted to show the people that were supposed to take care of me that I didn't need them.

Now, Piper is driving me crazy.

"That seems obvious," I tell her.

"You do it so people won't see the real you," she continues, ignoring me. Piper doesn't deal with my shit, and I like her all the more for it. "I think there's a big heart under there that you're afraid of letting people see."

"How do you know it's there?" My voice is rough now.

"Because you let me see it today."

"I…"

I don't even know what to say to her. Because I was open and honest with all of those kids at the hospital. They have no ulterior motives. They aren't trying to get something from you.

It's why I always say yes to team events like that, even when I refuse to participate in others.

"It's okay, Cash. You don't have to pretend it's not there."

I suck down more of my beer. "Tell me something else you like then."

It's an easy distraction to deflect from the emotions Piper is making me feel.

"Shortbreads are my favorite cookies, but I love making macarons. The science of it is definitely an art form. Amaryllis flowers are my favorite."

"The what? I don't think I've ever heard of that."

"They symbolize strength."

"What do you need strength for, Princess? You already seem to have it in spades."

She shakes her head. "Not always. It's a good reminder. I want it as a tattoo."

"Why haven't you gotten it yet?"

"I don't like needles. I need to work up the courage."

"Once you get one, they're addicting," I confirm.

I can only imagine ink marring her beautiful skin. Where would she have it? Somewhere only she could see? Somewhere others could?

"Which is your favorite tattoo?" Piper asks, breaking my thoughts before they go down the same dirty road as they have been all night.

"This one." I point to the crossed hockey sticks on my bicep with a date below it. "I got it after my first NHL goal."

"I like it."

Piper traces her fingers along the ink, sending goose bumps breaking out on my skin. The smallest touch from her affects me in ways I've never felt before.

I wish I could say I pull my head out of my ass, but I don't. The rest of the evening carries on like this. Her asking questions, fingers brushing my skin.

By the time I'm dropping her off at her car, I wish I could ask her to stay.

But I can't.

Hockey takes priority. I don't want to need people.

Needing people means you rely on them. Which always leads to them letting you down.

I've had enough letdowns for a lifetime.

"I'll see you at the arena tomorrow?" I ask Piper, shutting her door.

We each had one drink at the bar before switching to water. We talked for hours. I could tell you her preschool teacher's name at this point.

Easy, because it was her mother.

She nods.

"I'll be there."

Chapter Nine

"You're looking a little stiff there, Willy. You need a drink?" Troy asks.

I adjust my bow tie—not for the first time tonight—and look around. I don't think I've ever been invited to Cap's house before.

When Cassie told me and Piper that we had to be at the event tonight—to raise money for Team Rainbow, Angie's father's organization—Angie jumped at the chance to invite her for a day of pampering.

I'm just thankful that Piper's parents have a fundraiser at her mom's school so I won't meet them tonight. That would be way too much pressure on me.

"I'll take a beer if you have one." Anything to calm my nerves.

"Me too!" Noah chimes in from his spot on the couch.

"Coming right up."

I take the brief reprieve to look around Troy's living room. His house is like mine—nothing over-the-top or ostentatious. Angie and Troy live in one of the nicer areas of Denver and have a decent-sized back yard. Large

windows give them a view of downtown and the mountains beyond them. Everything in here looks cozy and lived
in. Likely Angie's doing. Nothing like mine that looks
straight out of a magazine.

"You nervous about tonight?" Noah asks.

I shrug a shoulder. "Not really."

"Then why do you look nervous?"

Noah is sitting there like he doesn't have a care in the
world.

"Because I have to hang out with you idiots all night."

"Ouch. That hurts." He mocks pain, throwing his
hand over his chest. "You wound me, Willy."

"Leave him alone. It's his first big night out with
Piper," Troy says, coming back into the room and handing
each of us a drink.

"It's still weird I didn't know you were dating my
sister." Noah shakes his head, sipping on the amber beer
Troy gave us.

"I'm a better option than Duncan," I tell him.

"He's not coming tonight, is he?" Noah asks.

I snort over the sip I took. "Hell no. The team didn't
mandate it, so he's probably off screwing his latest
conquest."

"What a dick," Troy says, dropping down onto the love
seat across from Noah. I take the seat next to him.

The fundraiser tonight isn't requiring the entire team
to be there. Me? Cassie told me that Piper and I have to
make an appearance.

To smile and play nice with the reporters that are
there. And because they all grew up together, Noah is
coming along as well, with Nick meeting us there. He said
something about not being able to hang out beforehand.

Whatever that means.

"At least we don't have to watch him schmooze all the

donors tonight," I say. "Sometimes I want to punch that look off his face."

Noah tilts his bottle at that. "Amen to that."

"Who do you want to punch?" That sweet voice filters into the room and I pop up from my seat, nearly sloshing my beer all over my tux.

And fuck me.

There's Piper.

Looking sexier than any person has the right to be.

Angie is walking over to Troy, but I don't spare her a second glance as Piper walks over to me.

"Who do you want to punch?" Piper asks again.

"Doesn't matter."

It's about all I can say because I can't string together any other coherent thoughts.

Piper is in a form-fitting black dress that flares out at her knees before it touches the ground. Her hair is styled in a fancy contraption that I couldn't even begin to name. A simple necklace sits on her collarbone, exposed from the strapless dress.

"Cat got your tongue?"

"God, I really need to get a date," Noah mutters to himself before heading out to the car that we hired for the night.

A smile dances across her face as her brother leaves the room.

It wouldn't surprise me if my tongue was hanging out of my mouth at this point, because I'm practically drooling over Piper.

The woman that is my girlfriend.

Fake girlfriend, you idiot, I chide myself.

It's hard to keep any sane thoughts when she looks so fucking stunning.

"You two ready to go?"

"What?"

My eyes shoot up at Troy's words. He has his arm wrapped around Angie's shoulders, keeping her by his side. She's in a red dress that's shorter in the front and longer in the back.

"Nothing. We need to get going."

Fucker.

"C'mon." I hold out my elbow to Piper, whose small hand drops into the crook. "You look beautiful."

"You don't look so bad yourself," Piper tells me, brushing a hand across the lapel of my tux.

The slightest touch from her makes me dizzy with need. I shouldn't be feeling this. Shouldn't even be *thinking* this. Especially with her brother in attendance tonight. But it's going to be hard to contain this…whatever it is for Piper.

At least no one at the event tonight will be able to tell it's fake, that's for sure.

PIPER

"CASH, do you support the team's charity initiatives?" a reporter asks him.

We arrived at the event to a slew of reporters hanging out. With this being a team event, they wanted to have all the local and national press here.

I know Cash hates it. In the few weeks we've been doing this thing, I've realized talking to the press is the worst part of his job.

If he could only play hockey and not have to deal with people, he'd love it.

He takes a minute before answering. My guess is to come up with an answer that won't be shitty toward said reporter.

"Of course I do," he tells them. "The charity tonight is one that is close to the team's heart. I love what they do to support inclusivity in sports. Something we should all work toward."

"It's a wonderful thing the Black Diamonds are doing with the gala to raise money." The reporter turns his eyes to me. I dig my fingers into Cash's hand and squeeze a bit harder. "And who is this on your arm?"

"Personal questions are off-limits," Cash snaps at him.

Squeezing his bicep, I drop into the perfect girlfriend role. I know Cash doesn't want to blast his personal life, but isn't this the whole point of me being here?

"I'm Cash's date for the evening." I don't give them any more information than that. Knowing them, they'll figure out exactly who I am within hours.

"And do you support the causes the team supports?"

Okay, what is it with these reporters? No wonder Cash hates them and their repetitive questions.

"I love the work the team does. I'm Denver born and raised, so the Black Diamonds are my team. Anything they do is a win in my book."

He nods along before moving on to the next person in line. Cash tugs at me as we head inside the double doors.

"That was a good answer."

"Thanks." I tilt my head up to look at him. "Hopefully that keeps them off your back."

A smile slips out before he covers it, shifting his hand to my back to escort me inside. A rush of heat flares up in me, but I do my best to ignore it.

The banquet hall of the event is expertly decorated. Guests in elegant formal wear linger among high-top tables with candles flickering. The lights are dim as servers weave in and out of the groups to offer champagne. Another offers small canapés. A silent auction table lines one wall while photos of Team Rainbow's work scroll on TVs spread through the room.

"Seems a bit extravagant," Cash whispers, his breath ghosting my ear. "A lot of this money probably could've gone to the organization itself."

"Do you know how much money they'll raise tonight?" I ask, my voice breathy.

"A shit ton." Cash is now smiling down at me. More butterflies are fluttering my belly. Damn my body and the reaction he causes in me. "That's why we're here."

Giving me a wink, he grabs a drink from a passing waiter and hands me the flute. Photographers are still milling about. Whether it's the for the press, the team, or whoever else, I know I need to put on a good face for Cash's benefit tonight.

Which was why Angie dragged me for a spa day to get ready for tonight. I'm so thankful she did. I would not have been prepared to come to something like this on my own.

I know my parents have been to events like this over the years since my dad is best friends with Alex Young, the founder of Team Rainbow, but I've never been.

And if it weren't for Cash, I wouldn't be here now.

For someone that doesn't like the press, he's good with people.

Surprisingly so.

Guests come up and talk to him about the season. About playing for the Black Diamonds. Where they were when the team won a Stanley Cup a few years ago.

Cash takes it all in stride. Shaking every hand and smiling for every picture that people ask for.

When there's a break, I take his hand and pull him over to a quiet corner.

"Think we'll get in trouble for this?" Cash asks, towering over me.

His presence in this small corner of the room is overwhelming.

"How are you feeling?" I ignore his question and press my hand to his chest. Warmth seeps out of him. So different from the Cash he displays to the world.

"Like I'm done with people for the next month."

I smile, brushing an imaginary piece of lint from the lapel of his suit. It's unfair how good he looks tonight.

The tux hides his tattoos. His hair is perfectly styled. Hell, Cash even shaved for tonight. He looks like a stand-up guy. One any team would be lucky to have.

And it's making my insides all swirly. Something that should definitely *not* be happening.

"Only a few more hours to go."

Cash takes a step forward, closing the distance between the two of us. His leather shoes touch the tips of my purple heels.

"I'm glad you're here with me tonight."

Cash's hand settles on my neck, thumb pressing against my pulse.

It's throbbing. Much like my lady parts right now.

He's so close, I can see how dark his eyes are, the light brown flecks disappearing into their depths. The way the tip of his tongue darts out to wet his lips.

I want him to kiss me. I want it more than anything. To feel what it's like to be under Cash's spell.

"Oh great. There you are!" Cassie's voice has Cash leaping away from me. "I have one more reporter I need you to talk to before dinner starts."

"Got it."

Cash shoves his hands into his pockets, trying not to look like he was caught.

"I appreciate you two coming tonight. Both of you." Cassie looks toward me, gaze drifting back to Cash before turning back to me.

"Didn't have a choice," Cash mumbles.

"I'm glad we could be here." I ignore the man standing next to me.

Cassie cuts him a glare. "I'm hearing wonderful things about the two of you. Keep it up."

"Anything for the team," Cash tells her.

His words are a bucket of cold water on whatever I was feeling.

Right. The team.

We're doing this for Cash and his place on the team.

No other reason and not because we're a real couple.

Now if I can only get that through my head.

Chapter Ten

CASH

> I figured it'd be good luck for tonight's game for you

> I like seeing you in my jersey <<sly face emoji>.

> Are you flirting with me?

> I must not be doing a good job if you're asking me that

> Maybe you should do it more often

> What the Princess wants, the Princess gets

> Then how about a hat trick tonight?

> You know it's hard for a defenseman to get one, right?

> Surprise me then

> I'll do what I can

"You've been grinning like an idiot all warm-up. What's with you?" Troy and Noah are standing in front of me.

"What's it to you guys?"

Noah waves a hand in front of me. I've never really noticed how much he and Piper look alike. They have the same easy smile that never seems to leave their face.

"Because you never smile this much," Troy tells me. "Is it because you're dating Piper?"

"I still can't believe you're dating Piper," Noah says. "She said she wouldn't date another player after Duncan."

Fuck. I never thought of having to win over her brother when Cassie concocted this crazy plan of hers.

"Well, she is."

"I don't know how you won her over," Nick says.

"What's with the twenty questions?" I grab my stick of deodorant and swipe on a liberal amount. Does he really have to bring this up before the game?

"Don't you know they're in love?" Duncan sneers from his locker across the room.

"Fuck off, Douche."

"I thought you were better than my sloppy seconds, Willy, but I guess not."

"You—"

I make to go after him, but Noah stops me in my tracks.

"Leave it be."

"Are you really going to let him talk about your sister like that?"

I flex my fingers and close them into a fist. What I wouldn't give to punch him across the face. Wipe that ever-present grin off his mouth.

"And risk getting suspended? He's not worth it."

"Fuck. Isn't Piper though?"

Noah shakes his head again. "She would tell you no too. You don't want to risk your spot on the team. Right?"

If Troy wasn't already captain, I'd say Noah was gunning for his position. He always knows exactly what to say to anyone on the team. His words deflate the balloon that expanded in my chest.

"I hate that he gets away with that shit."

I pull my gear on over my head and finish off with the navy and light-blue jersey. Of course Duncan stirs this shit up right before a game.

"I learned a long time ago that getting into fights isn't worth it. And Piper doesn't want you doing it either."

"How do you know that?"

"Because one of my teammates in college was hitting on her when she was still in high school. I lost my shit on him and almost got benched before a big-time scout was coming to see me play."

"What happened?" I twist the bandage around my fingers, taping them up.

"Piper went and told my coach what happened and the other guy got benched."

I snort out a laugh. "Of course she did." Because that sounds exactly like something Piper would do.

"See?" Noah slaps me on the shoulder. "She doesn't need us protecting her."

"I guess not," I grumble. I still wouldn't mind seeing someone take Duncan down a peg or two. Maybe a dozen, if I'm being honest.

"Does this mean you're bringing Piper to the team Thanksgiving dinner?" Troy asks.

"Say what now?"

"The annual team dinner before the holidays. You have to bring her."

I completely forgot about it. Because our schedule is crazy and we're starting a road trip the day before Thanksgiving, the team organizes a big dinner with the players and their families before we leave.

Bexley Hart, the team owner's daughter, loves putting it on. I usually never go because it's only me.

And it'd be pathetic to go on my own.

"I guess I am."

"Good." Noah is grinning like an idiot. "I can't wait to give her so much shit about this."

"Really, Strawberry?"

Noah groans at his nickname. The first day of practice, he walked in with a strawberry smoothie and somehow managed to drop the whole thing all over him. The name has stuck ever since.

"Yes. What good is having a little sister if you can't give her crap about who she's dating?"

Troy laughs. "My sister would kick my ass if I did that."

"Because she plays for the national team."

I don't know how Troy and his stepsister are both so gifted with hockey, but they are. It's one badass family.

"Cut the chitchat, gentlemen. It's time to get started," Coach Cooper barks at us.

"What's crawled up his ass lately?" I mutter.

"Don't get me started," Nick tells me. "He's been all over Piper and PT. Thinks she doesn't know a thing."

"Piper? She wouldn't be here if she didn't," I defend her.

"Hey, you don't have to tell me."

Coach Barney calls everyone's attention to him as we get ready for the game. About as easy of a win as they come by.

A 3-1 win over Detroit. The best way to head into the long holiday weekend.

※

"THANKSGIVING BEFORE THANKSGIVING?" Piper asks me as we head into the arena.

"We're leaving first thing tomorrow morning to play Arizona. We have to celebrate sometime."

"I think it's nice the team does this."

Piper is looking as gorgeous as ever in a nice pair of

black pants and a light-blue turtleneck sweater. Representing the Black Diamonds in a small way.

"I've never come."

"You haven't?"

"I've never wanted to leave Puck alone."

It's the lie I always tell, rather than that I don't have a family to bring with me. It's not something I want to tell people.

"I'm sure he could manage for a few hours."

I hold the door open for Piper as she brushes by me.

"You tell his cute little face no. It's harder than it looks."

Piper shakes her head. "That will not be me. He loves me."

"See? Not so easy."

By the time we get to the family suite, the place is packed. Most of the team is already here. Kids are running around, shouting as balloons are given to each of them. A paper turkey decorating station is set up in one corner and a bartender in another.

"Wow. They pull out all the stops."

Chafing dishes are set out with every kind of Thanksgiving food you could ask for. Turkey. Mashed potatoes. All different kinds of corn. Rolls. Vegetables. Pies. Cookies.

My mouth is watering just looking at it.

"Cash. I'm glad you could join us." Coach Barney comes up to the two of us. "And nice to see you outside of the arena, Piper. Well, in a more casual setting."

"I'm glad I could come," she tells him.

"Grab something to eat. The turkey is going fast."

"Thanks, Coach."

I shake his hand before guiding Piper to the buffet line.

"Angie!" Piper gives the woman in front of us a big hug. "I was hoping you'd be here."

"I was going to text, but I got busy with work this week."

Piper waves her off. "Don't worry about it."

The two of them start chatting away as Troy hands me a plate from the other side of the line. "When we told you to come, I thought you just said yes to get us off your back."

"I'm a man of my word." I take a small helping of turkey before piling on the sides.

Piper and Angie lead Troy and me to an empty table in the middle of the room.

"Do you have plans for real Thanksgiving?" Angie asks Piper.

"I'll be at my mom and dad's and we'll watch the game. Now with two guys playing, I'll have to keep an eye on them." She winks from her spot next to me.

"I think my dads were talking about having everyone over," Angie says.

"Any chance for all of them to get together." Piper rolls her eyes. "Do they not know they don't have to have an excuse?"

Troy laughs. "We're men, Piper. We always need one."

Angie pats Troy on the arm. "Says the guy who is always coming up with a reason to hang out with them."

"It's a shame it's not a home game. My dad would love to finally meet you, Cash," Piper tells me.

"Really?"

"Yeah."

"Willy, you look scared shitless. He's not that bad," Troy tells him.

"He doesn't bite," Piper says.

"Unless you're dating his daughter," I mutter, stuffing a forkful of mashed potatoes and turkey into my mouth.

I know Piper is playing this up, but even the thought of

meeting her family scares me. I'm not the kind of guy you bring home to meet the parents. I never have been.

Parents take one look at the tattoos and permanent scowl on my face and assume I'm going to break their daughter's heart. It was easier to never put myself in that situation.

Now doing it with Piper? Even if it's fake?

It has me sweating over the possibility of it.

"We're going to go make the rounds," Angie tells us.

Piper waves after her. "We'll try and meet up later."

By the time my head's back in the conversation, Troy and Angie are dumping their empty plates and heading off.

"Don't lose sleep over it, Cash. They'll love you," Troy says so only I can hear just before he walks away.

"Sure thing."

Piper grabs the two of us fresh drinks as we make our own rounds, running into people she knows from the physio room and some of the guys that I like on the team.

Thankfully, Duncan is not here. I wouldn't have the energy to put up with him tonight.

"Donation?" Nick asks, coming up to the two of us.

"For what?" Piper asks.

"The food bank. Bexley makes a donation for the holiday season, but we're getting the players to donate."

"We?" Piper quirks a brow at him as she pulls a twenty from her purse and drops it in the jar.

I pull out a small handful of bills and push them in.

"The Black Diamonds."

He's off to the next grouping of people before we can question him further.

Nick works his way through the crowd as a mic gets tapped, and we see Coach Barney has taken the mic from the DJ.

"I'd like to say a few words before we wrap up tonight.

We've had a great start to the season, and while I'm thankful for that, I'm mostly thankful for the great group of men we have in this room. We have some new guys here that we're sharing this tradition with. I know we all have lives outside of the rink—"

"We do?" someone yells from the back.

"I get it, I get it." Coach laughs. "But I want to thank the families for sharing their husbands and partners with us. It's not easy what we do. We're gone for long stretches, often missing birthdays, anniversaries, and holidays. So thank you for giving them to us so we can all play the game we love."

"You can have them longer if you need!" a wife pipes up from somewhere.

Laughter breaks out among the wives.

"Sorry. It's time for you to have them back. If you're a Black Diamond, time for curfew."

Everyone breaks out into laughter at Coach's final words.

It has its intended effect, breaking up the party. Guys start gathering kids and heading out.

"We'll catch a drink this week," Angie tells Piper. "Nice seeing you, Cash."

"You too."

The drive back to Piper's place is quiet, both of us lost in our thoughts.

Tonight was fun. Something I didn't think I'd have.

Piper fits in easily with these people. Too easily.

I've been alone for so long; I don't know how to bring someone into my life. I made room for Puck because the team hosted an adoption event a few years ago. I couldn't say no to his face.

"Thanks for a great night, Cash."

"Night, Princess.

"Piper, would you mind getting the ice baths ready? A few guys are coming in after practice."

"Sure thing, Claire."

It's not the most glamorous job, but I don't mind. It's all part of what I need to do in order to get my degree.

Will I work in hockey in the future? I don't know. I'd love to do something with sports because that's what I've grown up around, but who knows?

I haul buckets of ice into the cold, metal tubs so they'll be ready for the guys.

Nick is the first one in.

"Hey. How was practice?"

"Good." He nods, chugging from his water bottle. "Feels good to be back between the pipes."

"I don't envy you at all."

"What, you don't want to take a puck flying at you at ninety miles per hour?"

I wince. "There's no way I could. I'd get scared and duck."

Nick laughs, a quiet sound because he hates being the

center of attention. "It's a good thing you aren't playing for us then."

Sliding into the tub, Nick lets out a loud gasp.

"How ya' feeling?"

"I'll be better when I'm out."

"You know it helps," I chastise him.

"Doesn't mean I don't hate it."

"Put your big-boy pants on," I tell him as I laugh and get the next one ready.

Duncan and another teammate walk in. This is why I shouldn't date players. Because I have to see them when we break up.

I focus my attention on the various equipment around the room. No sense in getting worked up because of Duncan.

"You good?" Nick asks.

I smile at him. One I don't really feel. "I'm good."

I hate that Duncan still has this pull over me. Not that I still have feelings for him, but God, what a dick.

"Ava is crazy in bed." Duncan has a smug look on his face as he gets into the tub. "Gives any guy a zamboner."

I spin away, organizing a stack of towels so I don't have to see him. God, what a tool.

Not that I care that they're still seeing each other. Those two deserve each other.

"I thought you weren't seeing her anymore?" someone asks Duncan. I don't know who.

"And give up that kind of sex? Hell no."

"Man, you get all the ladies. I don't know how you do it."

"She's great if you need a quick lay. No one will say no to me."

More like she wants to bag a hockey player. But I keep that to myself.

"I need to learn at your feet. You get more ass than anyone I know."

"Damn straight."

I fight the groan. What did I ever see in Duncan? Did he talk about me like this with the team? I hate to think about it. I don't want anyone knowing anything about our sex life.

At least it's not something I have to worry about now.

"Maybe Ava has some friends you can hook me up with."

"Oh God," I mutter to myself. I hate that I have to subject myself to this conversation.

"Need something, Piper?" I hear Duncan chirp.

I turn toward his smarmy voice. "No. Do you have everything you need?"

I paste an extra big smile on my face. It's the only way I can deal with him.

"Hey, maybe you can hook me up with Piper."

My eyes fly to the guy in the tub that I'm not too familiar with.

Rhodes? Riley? I should know who he is since he's glommed onto Duncan, but I don't.

I only work with a handful of players, so I'm not on a first-name basis with all the guys. He has slicked back, dark hair. No doubt from practice. A scar cuts through his jaw.

Nothing about this guy is attractive.

Although, I question my sanity because I found Duncan attractive.

"Nah. You don't want her." Duncan looks me square in the eye, dripping water as he gets out of the ice bath. I refuse to back down from him. I want to know what he's going to say after that.

"Why not?" Riley/Rhodes/whoever asks.

There's a slight lilt to his lips as he answers. "She's not good in bed."

My entire head is buzzing with anger. I'm seeing red. Shaking. I'm so pissed at the words I couldn't have possibly heard come out of Duncan's mouth.

"Are—"

The words die on my tongue as Cash comes barreling into the room, heading straight for Duncan.

"What the fuck is wrong with you?"

Duncan and Cash are chest to chest. Looking at the two of them up close, Cash towers over my ex.

More muscle.

More solid.

More…everything.

"What's it matter to you?" Duncan sneers. "Your girlfriend can't take a little criticism?"

"A little criticism?" Cash's hand flexes into a fist at his side. "You're being a fucking asshole. That's what you are. You don't talk about Piper—hell, any woman—that way."

"What's a little locker-room talk between teammates?" Duncan tries to brush off Cash's words.

"Apologize. Now." Cash's mouth barely moves. I can feel the anger rolling off him in waves.

Grabbing Cash's shoulder, I step between him and Duncan. My small stature has never been more apparent than standing between these two hulking men.

"I'm sorry you feel the need to cast aspersions about our sex life, Duncan, but I can assure you, that's not how it actually happened."

I surprise myself by being able to get the words out. At how calm I sound.

Duncan looks confused. "What are you talking about, Piper?"

I go in for the kill. Because if this man is going to treat

me like this, I'm going to share the details. Even if these guys don't need to know it. Duncan doesn't get to have the upper hand here after what he did to me.

Fuck being the bigger person.

"Not good in bed? I had to get myself off every time we had sex together. Could never seem to make a woman finish, could you?"

Cash's warm hand settles on my hip, giving me a squeeze. Knowing he's behind me instills more confidence in me as I watch the anger wash over Duncan's face.

"Dude, are you serious?" one of the guys asks.

I glance around at them. "Sorry. Your little sex god here isn't all he's cracked up to be."

"Are you really going to listen to her?" Duncan tries to save face. "I bet Cash here doesn't get her off either."

"Wouldn't you like to know?" I cross my arms over my chest, staring him down. "He's more of a man than you'll ever be."

"I doubt it."

I make a split-second decision. Cash's face makes it clear he is still angry at Duncan, but he's also staring at me with confusion.

Clasping Cash around the neck, I pull him down to me and lay one on him.

Shock is the only way to describe how he's reacting right now. Cash's lips are firm, unmovable, under mine.

Oh God. I completely misread this situation.

Except…is Cash kissing me back?

CASH

Oh shit. I should not be doing this. I should not be

kissing Piper. But when I came into the training room after practice and heard what Duncan said about her?

I nearly lost my shit.

A few of the guys on the team will talk about people like that, but Piper?

I was lucky Piper decided to kiss me instead of my punching Duncan and getting cut for behavior detrimental to the team.

But I don't care about that. Not when Piper's soft-as-clouds lips are on mine.

And taste as sweet as vanilla.

My hands wrap around her waist and pull her in close.

I shouldn't be doing this. Kissing her like this.

Kissing leads to feelings. Feelings neither one of us needs to have.

I don't care about any of that right now as I deepen the kiss. As I sweep my tongue into Piper's mouth.

She likes it, if her fingertips digging into the short strands of hair on the back of my neck are anything to go by.

The training room completely fades away as I get lost in Piper. Everything about her is invading my senses.

Her sweet taste.

The way she smells.

How soft her curves feel under my hands.

Piper Fields could drive a sane man wild.

Me?

I am feral.

I have no sanity. Not when it comes to her. I've lost it when it comes to the woman in my arms.

"Get a room," someone calls out, breaking the trance I'm in.

Pulling back ever so slightly, my gaze connects with

hers. Her lips are wet, and all I want to do is take them again. Blue eyes filled with lust are staring up at me.

The one thing I don't see there?

Regret.

Good. Because the last thing I want is for her to feel remorse about this. Fuck. I don't think I ever could with kissing her.

"You okay?" I cup her cheek.

She looks around, before nodding at me. I glance around the now-empty training room. It's only the two of us. I should step back and give her some space, but I don't want to.

Turns out, I like having Piper in my arms.

"Yeah." She blows out a breath. "Thank you for coming to my defense."

I shake my head. "I would have punched the living daylights out of him if it weren't for you."

"I can't believe he said that."

I smirk down at her. "I think you were holding your own pretty well."

"I don't think everyone on the team needed to know about me and my vibrator."

This time, shock hits me square in the chest and I take a step back. "You mean…that was real?"

A blush creeps up Piper's cheeks. It wasn't there when she told Duncan about it, but I can only imagine now.

"Yes." Her voice is firm. "If he can talk about me that way, I can most certainly spill the beans on him."

Fuck. Me.

This is the very last thing I need to be picturing. The sexy-as-fuck woman standing in front of me using her vibrator to get off.

Is it purple? Pink? Blue?

What's her O-face look like?

"Earth to Cash."

Piper is snapping her fingers in front of my face.

"Sorry."

"Are *you* okay?" she asks me.

"Me? He's the one that was trying to embarrass you in front of everyone."

"He has small dick syndrome. He has to make up for it somehow." She shrugs a shoulder.

Her words have me bursting into laughter. "Damn, Princess. You're brutal."

"I mean, have you seen his dick?" She holds her fingers a few inches apart, nothing sizable. "There isn't much to work with there."

"Is this how you talk about all your boyfriends' dicks?" I ask, quirking a brow at her. I lean my ass against the massage table.

Piper takes a tentative step toward me. "Not everyone."

"No?"

Is she talking about me now?

"I haven't talked about yours."

This is a conversation I shouldn't have started. Two minutes after kissing Piper and my brain is mush.

"Because you don't have any clue what you're dealing with."

Her eyes flit down to my crotch, and I know she's thinking about it now.

Just like I am.

I don't know if all that sweetness could handle my pierced dick. How long it gets when I'm hard. Kind of like now—just thinking about her taking it.

"Think you could handle it? Handle my cock?"

Piper's eyes snap to meet mine. She doesn't flinch at my words. Hmm. Maybe she could handle it.

"Guess we'll never know."

Piper bounds out of the training room in a whiff of perfume that goes straight to my groin.

Fuck. I rub the heel of my hand over my dick to try and stave off coming in my pants.

The Princess has cast her spell over me. I don't know if I'll ever be able to break it.

Chapter Twelve

PIPER

You have good taste too. Maybe I'll have some special treats you can take home to Puck

Any treats for me?

Guess you'll have to come and find out

I'll be there at seven

"I don't know why I'm so nervous."

"Maybe because it's the first time he's coming over to your apartment," Angie tells me over the phone. "If you've only ever been to his place, it's natural."

Ever since I've started going to more team events as Cash's girlfriend, Angie and I have been talking a lot more. Not that we never talked before—since our dads are best friends—but I always felt like the annoying little kid tagging along.

"My place is so much smaller than his."

"He'll fit right in. Stop worrying, Piper."

I look around the small studio apartment that I moved into after Ava bailed on me.

Well, not bailed. There was no way I was going to let her stay with me after she was screwing my boyfriend.

It's tiny, not a whole lot to it, but I've made it my own.

Plants line the windowsill. Oversized pillows sit perfectly fluffed on the couch with a soft purple throw. Photos of flowers and the mountains cover the bright white walls. The small kitchen is hidden from my bedroom by a curtain with the bathroom by the front door.

I wish there was more room for odds and ends, but I don't want it too crowded. Could I get a bigger place? Yes.

But this was the first one on my budget that I could get on such short notice.

Especially with not knowing what I'm going to be doing after I graduate next spring.

"Look, it'll be fine. I promise." Angie brings my attention back to our call. "Better than being out in public if you want some privacy."

"Angie!" I hiss. "You can't say things like that!"

"Why not? You deserve fun, Piper. You've been through a lot."

"And I'm hanging up now."

I end the call just as a knock sounds from the door. I smooth a hand down my simple purple sweater and head to the door. Nothing overly fancy tonight—just jeans and a sweater since we're staying in.

After a long day of helping at the training center, I really didn't want to do anything more than this.

Plus, I figure Cash likes fewer prying eyes on him.

I pull open the door, and Cash is standing there in all his glory.

And oof, what a glory it is.

Tall. Broad. He leans against the door, filling the space. Cash has a presence about him that I can't get used to.

"You just going to stand there, or are you going to let me in?"

"Oh, sorry." His voice startles me as I open the door for him to walk in.

Cash brushes by me on his way inside. He smells like fresh soap. A smell I've never noticed before, but that fits him.

Clean. Efficient.

Just like everything he does.

My apartment seems smaller with him in it. He shrugs out of his jacket and I drink my fill.

A tight black T-shirt clings to his muscles. The gray joggers he's wearing hug his strong thighs.

He toes out of his tennis shoes and pushes them against the wall.

God, he really is the sexiest man alive.

And I hate that I keep thinking that every time I'm around him.

"So, what are we making tonight?" Cash rests his forearms on the small counter space that I have.

"We're baking cookies."

"What kind?"

"Chocolate chip."

He smirks. "Why not shortbread?"

"Look at you paying attention."

Cash walks around the counter and pulls me close to him. "I pay attention to you, Princess."

I get lost in his eyes. Big, brown pools that are open to me. They are telling me everything I need to know about this man right now.

That he's feeling things for me. Things I'm *also* feeling for him.

Neither of us makes a move to leave the other's arms.

"We should get started." Cash's voice is deep. Deeper than I've ever heard it. I want to hear it whispering sweet nothings in my ear. Calling me Princess as he sinks inside of me.

I shake the thoughts from my head and turn to the pantry. "Let me get you an apron."

"An apron?"

"I don't want you making a mess."

I grab the purple apron covered in macarons and drape it over Cash's neck. I reach around him to tie it, letting my fingers linger on him.

"How do I look?" He cocks an eyebrow at me. Brown hair falls over his eyes.

A giggle escapes me as I take him in. "You look ridiculous."

"Alright, alright. Let's get started."

"Wait. I need to snap a picture to post."

"Right." Cash clears his throat. "Good idea."

Those corners of his mouth pull into a small smile.

"Now, we need to follow the instructions closely."

I already have all the ingredients laid out. I step up next to Cash, the two of us moving things around.

"So why are we making cookies?"

I hand him a measuring cup. "Tomorrow is Claire's birthday, so we're having a small potluck at lunch."

"That's nice of you."

"And nice you're volunteering to help."

"I might not be much help with cooking. I never did much of it."

"Too busy with hockey?"

"Yeah."

The way Cash says it has me thinking he's not telling me the whole truth. But I'll let him slide tonight.

"My mom and I did a lot of baking when I was growing up. She loved being the team mom for Noah's hockey team, so I got to help with the cookies."

"That sounds nice."

Cash focuses on measuring out the sugar. His tongue peeks out from his lips, and I can't help but snap another photo.

"What?" he asks, looking up.

"Nothing. You look cute."

"I'm not cute," he grumbles.

"Oh yeah? Then what are you?"

I hop up onto the counter and grab the tub of flour.

"Puck is cute. I'm a sex god."

I burst out laughing, covering my mouth with my hand to try and rein it back in.

"A sex god?"

"Why are you laughing?" Cash throws the spoon down on the counter.

"You went from cute to sex god on quite a leap there, sex god."

"I can't have you thinking I'm cute."

I bite my lip to keep my words from spilling out. That he's way more than cute. I don't know if he's a sex god, but I'd like to see his moves in action.

I don't tell him that though.

Instead, I focus on the flour. Except the bin is too full and a puff of it comes exploding out when I pull the lid off.

It settles all over both of us, coating Cash's hair and face and falling onto my legs and arms.

"Okay, can I say you look cute now covered in flour in that apron?"

Cash laughs, an unfamiliar sound but one that washes over me and takes hold. I want to hear more of it. It's an easy sound.

"Was this your plan the whole time?" He tries to wipe it from his eyes, but only pushes it around.

"Hang on. We need to document this."

I spin Cash and wrap an arm around his shoulders. Flipping the camera onto us, I snap a photo.

What I see on the tiny screen surprises me. Cash's lips are tilted up into a smile. Flour coats both of us, some still floating through the air.

If I didn't know any better, I'd say we were a real couple.

"Send that to me."

"Why?" I ask.

"So I can post it too."

Right. Posting. I nearly forgot.

"Everyone is going to love this."

I send it to Cash and make a quick post about cooking with my boyfriend.

"The bad boy of the Black Diamonds covered in flour?"

I bark out a laugh and reach over to grab a paper towel to clean ourselves up. "Is that what you call yourself?"

He shakes his head, stepping between my legs.

"No. But it's how people see me. So maybe a little flour will help soften the image."

"Sweeten you up," I tell him.

"I don't think I need cookies for that."

"Why not?"

Cash leans in closer. The stubble along his jaw looks soft. I want to feel it under my hands.

"I have you for that."

Cash leans in close, taking my lips in the kiss to end all kisses. I'm prepared for a reckless assault. For him to kiss me like he plays hockey. With a force that he can't seem to contain.

How he's kissing me now? It's with a softness I wasn't expecting. A brush of his lips as he opens my mouth with his tongue. Heat gathers in my core as I cling to him. I want to feel every bit of him. Of this kiss.

Cash Williams is going to drive me wild with these kisses. He pulls me to the edge of the counter, tilting my head and deepening the angle. I give in to him. Let him have complete control as my body falls under his spell.

Rough hands slip under my T-shirt. It feels like heaven. I want to peel off every layer and let him have his way with me.

Except…

"Show me," he whispers against my neck.

"What?" My brain is in a kiss-induced fog.

"How you get yourself off."

I pull back, staring at the man in front of me.

Instead of saying anything, I hop off the counter and saunter toward my bed.

Because if Cash wants to see me get myself off, he gets what he wants.

Chapter Thirteen

CASH

Piper downright sashays to her bed, swinging those hips of hers on the way. My cock is ready to punch his way out of my boxers.

I couldn't help the words as they left me. But all I can think about now is the woman who is peeling her sweater off and dropping it on the floor.

Exposing her bare back to me.

"Fuck."

Piper peers at me over her shoulder. "Are you just going to stand there all night?"

I close the distance in two strides. Thank God for her shoebox of an apartment.

I press a line of kisses along her collarbone. Her nipples are tight and perky.

"Ready for me?"

My free hand closes over her small tit and gives it a squeeze.

"Yes!" she gasps.

"Good."

I release her and take a step back, leaning against the small wall that divides the bedroom and living room.

Piper walks around her bed and pulls open her nightstand drawer. The contraption she takes out is purple, with a large head and bumps covering the length. A set of what looks like tentacles stick out from it.

"Look at you, Princess."

"What can I say? I like to have fun in bed."

"Fuck." I rub myself through my joggers. If she keeps this up, I'm going to blow a load in my pants.

Piper throws it on the bed and then undoes her jeans and steps out of them. She's in a pair of simple black underwear, but she makes them sexy.

"You going to take those off?"

Kneeling on the bed, Piper moves toward the center and lies down. "Why don't you help me with them?"

"I think I can do that."

Leaning over her, I press a kiss just below her belly button. I want time to explore all of this beautiful body. But right now, I want to see what she does with the toy on her bed.

I peel the soft fabric down her legs and take a whiff of them. "You're already wet for me, Princess."

"I can't help it when you're around."

I shove the material in my joggers pocket. No way am I letting her have these back.

Piper grabs the small bottle of lube and coats the purple plastic, then flicks the switch on. The buzzing echoes around the small studio.

Dragging the dildo down her stomach, Piper slides it between her folds. "Gah!"

"Fuck. Fuck." I can't contain myself anymore. I shove my own hand down my pants to stroke myself.

"Not yet."

"What?"

Piper looks up at me as she slides the vibrator through her pussy.

"You don't get to touch yourself. Not until I say so."

"Shit." I pull my hand out, wishing I could have more. But it makes it that much hotter as Piper pushes the thing inside her.

"I picture you."

"What?"

I'm only capable of speaking in one-syllable words. All rational thought has fled my brain at watching Piper get herself off.

"When I masturbate. I picture you."

"Fuck." I want to touch myself. To stroke myself off at her words.

"The way you skate. How powerful you are. How sexy you are."

"Piper," I growl. "You're killing me."

She sinks the device in deeper, spreading her legs wide so I can see. I don't think I've ever seen anything so sexy in my life.

Her pussy is glistening with her need as she moves it in and out.

"You're killing me, Princess."

"Do it."

"Thank fuck."

I don't waste any more time, shoving my joggers and boxers down my legs. My cock springs free, slapping me in the stomach. Blue eyes widen as I kneel between her legs.

"It's—"

"Yup. Pierced."

The metal barbells line the top of my shaft. Piper licks her lips as I give myself lazy strokes.

"I've never been with someone so...big."

I shift closer, resting a hand by her head and hovering over her. "You'd take it like a good girl. Feeling every piercing inside you. Letting a real man get you off."

"You always get me off."

"Oh yeah? How do I do that?"

Piper closes her eyes as she arches off the bed. She's getting close to coming, and I can't fucking wait to see her explode.

"With your tongue. You're a master at eating me out."

"Oh, believe me, Princess. I will make you come on my tongue several times before you even get to my cock."

"Yes!" She squirms even more beneath me. "I'm not even done coming before you're pushing inside me. Bare. No condoms."

My motions pick up. The thought of being inside this pretty pussy with nothing between us is almost too much to take.

"I'm negative. We can make that happen."

Piper's eyes fly open to meet mine. "Me too. And I'm on the pill."

"I'll remember that." I nod down to her and cover her hand with mine, pushing the vibrator deeper inside her. The vibrations pulse through me as the tentacles play with her clit. "Now, keep going. Tell me how you come for me."

"You flip me onto all fours. Slapping my ass as you play with my clit."

"Fuck, Piper." I grunt. I'm ready to come all over her, but she's not there yet.

"You call me Princess. You bend over me, covering my body with yours."

I can picture it in my head. All of my tattoos against her pure white skin. Like I'm defiling the woman below me.

God, I wish it were my own cock inside of her right now.

"You look so fucking sexy from here."

Piper tries to pull it out, but I hold her hand still. "I need you to come."

"Don't stop."

All the blood rushes south. I'm so fucking hard, I could die if I don't come right now. Watching as the two of us get Piper off is the hottest thing I've ever experienced.

"Cash!" Piper screams and I know she's coming.

I shoot off right there with her, exploding into a tiny thousand pieces.

"Fuuuuck."

Ropes of cum coat Piper's hand. Her arm. Stomach. Landing on her tits.

My skin is on fire as I stay focused on the woman below me. A blush creeps over her skin as her grip slackens on the vibrator. Sitting back on my heels, I pull it out of her and turn it off.

"Let me—"

"Come here." Piper pulls me toward her.

I lie next to her, wrapping my arms around her. Our legs are all twisted up together as our breaths mingle.

"How are you feeling?" I drop a kiss onto her head. Piper's fingers drift up and down my chest.

"Surprised."

"Surprised you could come that hard?" I laugh.

"Surprised at your dick."

"Good surprise or bad surprise?" I ask.

"Good. Very good." Piper rests her chin on my chest and stares up at me. "I need to recover before I let you fuck me."

"You're killing me, Princess." I tuck a lock of soft, blonde hair behind her ear.

"Next time, Cash."

"Promise me."

There's no way I can let this be the only time I experience Piper like this. Now that I know what she looks like when she comes, I want everything.

Every kiss. Every moan. Every whimper. Every orgasm she has from now until the end.

Whenever the end is for the two of us.

"C'mon, Princess. Let's get you cleaned up."

"I like that you call me Princess."

I start the shower and hold her in my arms.

"Yeah?"

Closing her eyes, she rests against my chest. "Yeah. Like I'm yours."

"You are, Princess. You are."

Whether she believes me or not, it's true.

Piper is mine.

Chapter Fourteen

"You ready for the game tonight?" Troy asks, dropping down onto the padded leather bench seat next to me.

"Of course I'm fucking ready tonight. Why wouldn't I be?"

"I don't know. You've been in the media a lot lately."

"And by being in the media, do you mean me and Piper?"

Troy gives me a sheepish grin. "Well, you have been, haven't you?"

Not that I'm going to tell Troy this, but it's been very, very well received from Cassie. "Hey, just because we're in the press doesn't mean my head's not in the game for tonight."

"Boston's a tough team. I know what we need to do tonight." Troy elbows me in the side.

"Good, because I don't want to lose to this team again."

"Trust me, man, we're not going to." I pull the eighty-one jersey down over my pads and get ready for the game, taking a few deep breaths.

Now that Piper has started coming to games more often than she was, I want to impress her. When I was a kid, the only way I could get my parents' attention was to get into fights. Piper doesn't care about that. She likes it when I play well. Especially since she told me how worked up it gets her.

. If I could score every goal for her, I would.

We've only been doing this whole fake dating for a few weeks, but I'm quickly becoming addicted to her. Piper was waiting for me in my bed last night when I slipped in from another late game. I didn't have the heart to wake her up when I got in, or this morning before her class, so I left a sticky note for her.

DIDN'T WANT TO WAKE YOU BEFORE I LEFT, SLEEPING BEAUTY. I'LL SEE YOU AT THE GAME TONIGHT
   XO CASH

Coach Barney gives us his usual words of wisdom before the game, and I follow the guys out onto the ice for a quick warm-up before the pregame festivities.

My eyes automatically track up to the family suite—where all the WAGs are. The fact that I know Piper's going to be wearing my jersey again tonight makes me that much more turned on, which I shouldn't be because I'm getting ready to play sixty minutes of hockey.

"What are you smiling about?" Duncan asks.

Of course Duncan skates up next to me the moment I smile. Something that isn't all that familiar on my face.

Ever since Piper came into my life though, it's becoming a more regular occurrence.

"Nothing that concerns you, asshole."

"Oh look, maybe you should get laid by your sweet new little girlfriend. Piper, is it?"

"You know exactly who my girlfriend is, Douche. I don't want to hear her name come out of your mouth ever again."

"Oh, and what are you going to do about it if I do?"

Nothing that I can do to him right now. We're out on the ice for warm-ups. To anyone in the crowd, it'd look like we're chatting about the game. He winks at me as he skates away.

What a fucker. I hope he gets what's coming to him. He is about as far from a Black Diamond as they come. He doesn't fit the standard the team holds everyone to. Duncan uses his position on the team to get anything he wants.

I do my best to push Duncan out of my mind. He doesn't need to be my focus right now. Instead I need to be thinking about Boston and trying to beat them.

From the minute the puck drops, it's a battle.

Boston takes no prisoners as they skate all over us. No matter how hard we fight, we can't clear the puck from our zone. I'm pushing myself, but they still manage an easy goal. The kind I hate letting get by me. The anger radiating off Nick is palpable as he slams his stick into the goal.

"We'll get it back," I tell him, standing next to him. The hometown fans are booing their displeasure.

"We will."

"Keep your head up." I bump him with my stick in his pads before heading to the bench.

Except we don't. By the time the first period ends,

we're down by two. The way things are going, we are lucky it's not worse.

"All right, boys. That first period was not how we wanted it to go. Just because we're down by two doesn't mean we lie down and give up."

Coach B looks across the locker room. Heads are hanging while other guys are icing various aches and pains.

"I want you to put that 'we're down and out' mentality out of your heads right now. We don't need that right now. We have forty more minutes to play. Get your heads on straight so we can go out there and take this win from them."

"You heard Coach Barney!" Troy shouts, hopping up from his spot on the bench. "Don't let one bad period get to you. We've got this. Let's get back out there and bring this game home!"

Troy's words send a pulse of excitement through the locker room. Guys are getting pumped up as we head back out to start the second period.

This time, I'm on the ice when the puck drops. Troy grabs it easily and skates toward the Boston end of the ice. A defenseman blocks Troy's shot and shoots it to their winger.

I'm ready for them. Skating backward, I watch the two of them as they skate into our zone. I make my move to get the puck from them, but Boston is ready.

One of their guys seems to come out of nowhere and slams me into the boards.

"Fuck!" I yell out, dropping like a rag doll onto the ice.

Fuck. Pain is radiating out from my side as the whistle blows. The ref skates over as do a few of the other guys on our team.

I can't hear anything over the dull roar in my head. I push up onto my knees before getting back on my skates.

Did I break my ribs? This is not what I need to be dealing with right now.

"Willy, you okay?" Troy asks as I make my way to the bench.

"Fuck, it hurts."

"Think you can keep going?"

"Just need a minute." I nod.

I breathe through the pain as the door to the bench swings open.

"Cash, tell me how you're feeling," the trainer asks.

"Can't say I've felt this good in a while." I grimace, my joke falling flat as I try to suck in a deep breath.

"We're going to take you back for some X-rays to see if anything is broken."

I shake my head. "It's fine. I can play through it."

"Get checked out. I don't want you to hurt yourself any more," Coach Barney tells me. "We need you out there."

"Fine," I grumble.

The trainer helps me back to the locker room as the crowd starts to clap for me.

I don't want their applause right now. All I want is to get taped up to get back on the ice. Boston is too dominant of a team to let them get another goal on us. Hopefully with the power play, we'll be able to close the gap.

The trainer helps me with my pads. Even lifting my jersey up and over my head hurts my side.

"Pretty gnarly bruise forming here," he tells me.

"Gnarly? Is that your official assessment?" I ask as I get situated on the table.

I look down, seeing a purple and black bruise blossoming on my side. Unless a damn rib is poking out of me, I'm getting back on that ice tonight.

I try to take small, even breaths to calm down as the

machine does what it's supposed to. I hate that I'm in here and not out on the ice helping my team.

"Alright, Cash. Nothing is broken."

"Thank fuck." I blow out a breath. "Tape me. I need to get back out there."

"You need to be careful." He pierces me with a fierce look. "I mean it. Don't go out there gunning to hit anyone."

"I won't."

He makes quick work of taping me up and helping me get back into my pads and jersey. I pop a few ibuprofen he hands me before heading back toward the ice.

The cheers that hit my ears as I get closer can only mean one thing. By the time I find my place, we've tied the game up.

Thank fuck.

"You good?" Noah asks, leaning over a few of our teammates.

"Ready to get back out there."

"Good man." Coach Barney claps me on the shoulder from behind.

I'm only in the game for a few minutes this period. Boston does their best to try and get another goal, but we're playing with a strength that was missing in the first period.

The rest of the period runs out and we're in the final intermission. I slink into the locker room and collapse into my stall.

"You think you have one more period in you?" Troy asks, standing above me.

"You know I do. Just need to recoup for a few."

"No rest for the wicked." Troy laughs.

The trainer takes a few minutes to check out my tape, making sure I'm ready to go for the last period.

From the time we hit the ice, we're on the attack. Boston gets an easy goal but we answer with one of our own.

It's a constant back and forth. No one is giving up. Noah and Troy are working hard when one of them passes the puck to me.

One of our guys blocks Boston and it gives me an opening.

I fight through the pain, flying down the ice. Out of the corner of my eye, I see one of our guys block a Boston player, and it's just me and the goalie.

I watch his glove drop a fraction and I fire, watching the puck pass through the small space between his glove and the bar.

Hearing that horn blare might be the best sound ever.

"Fuck yeah!" I cheer as the guys all pile on around me.

"Amazing goal, Willy!" Troy claps me on the helmet.

"Damn straight!" I tell him, smiling like a fool as I skate back to the bench. I don't feel an ounce of pain right now. With a minute left, we need to run the clock out and hope like hell Boston can't put the biscuit between the pipes.

The energy is palpable as the seconds tick away. Our guys are fighting hard. The last thing I want is to go into OT. All I want is to collapse into bed with Piper right about now.

And as the clock hits zero, it's our game. We squeeze out the win, 4-3.

The entire team heads into the locker room. The mood is jubilant. Boston is not an easy team to beat, so it's lively as music plays from someone's locker.

"Cash, got a few minutes?" Weber asks. A few reporters are already in the locker room talking to the guys.

"Sure thing."

"First off, how are you feeling?"

"I've been better."

"It was a hard hit into the boards. You came back and were able to seal the win for the Black Diamonds."

I nod. "The guys did a great job keeping us in the game."

"You did too. That goal was a thing of beauty."

"Thanks, Franklin. It wouldn't have happened if Noah and Troy hadn't set me up."

"How are you going to celebrate the win?"

"Boston is a tough team, so I'm going to enjoy it and then buckle down and focus on the next game. Take the time to rest up so I'm ready."

"Thanks, Cash."

Weber leaves and I hit the showers. Adrenaline from the game was carrying me through the night, but now exhaustion is settling in.

I don't waste any time because all I want right now is to go home. I know I'll need to check in with the trainers, but I want to sleep.

With Piper in my arms.

Heading back to my locker, I grab my phone and am met with a slew of messages.

PRINCESS

Are you okay?! That hit was crazy! He should have been kicked out of the game. Five minutes for boarding?! Please! Kick his ass out!

Not me sitting here biting my nails waiting on an update from the team…

You're back!

> Are you able to play still?

> Of course you are. You're on the ice

> That goal! Cash! OH. MY. GOD. <<excited gif here>>

> I can't wait to see you <<kissing emoji>>

A LAUGH ESCAPES me as I read all of her texts. I fire one off back to her.

CASH

> I need to get checked out again. Meet me at home? Puck will be happy to see you

HER RESPONSE IS IMMEDIATE.

> Okay <3

AFTER GETTING CHECKED out and changing into street clothes, I walk out to find Cassie waiting for me outside the locker room. "There's the hero of the hour."

"Nah." I brush off her praise. "Anyone would have been able to do that."

Cassie pats me gingerly on the arm. "Not anyone. You're a great player, Cash, and to do it with an injury? That was incredible."

"Thanks." I throw a thumb behind me toward the players' parking lot. "I need to head out."

"Piper?"

I nod.

Cassie gives me a look of understanding. "She's good for you, Cash."

I wish that I could deny that she is, but I don't think this change would have come with just anyone.

"I like her."

"Only a few more weeks, Cash, and then you can have your life back." Cassie leaves me behind, thinking on her words.

I've never needed anyone. Needing someone makes you weak. Having people in your life just means it hurts when they leave.

But Piper? I don't know how to keep her.

That's a problem for future me. Right now, I just want to have her in my arms.

Chapter Fifteen

"Puck?" I let myself into Cash's house using the code to the garage he gave me. "Where are you?"

Skittering paws against the hardwood floor greet me as Puck runs to me, tongue hanging out of his mouth. The TV is quietly playing highlights from the game.

I smile. Cash never likes Puck feeling left alone, so he always has the TV on for him. Playing his game, no doubt.

"Hi, sweet boy. Did you have a good night?" I get down on my knees to accept his kisses. "Your dad should be home soon."

He barks at me, running to the back door.

Dropping my keys onto the counter, I follow him and let him out into the cold night air.

Puck runs around, sniffing at all the things he likes.

I'm anxious to see Cash. I didn't see him today because I had an exam. I don't think I've ever seen him take a hit like that. Hockey is a brutal game. The guy from Boston hit him with a force I haven't seen. My heart was in my throat the entire time Cash wasn't on the ice.

As someone who works with the guys and injuries, my mind kept going to the worst-case scenario.

Broken ribs?

Punctured lung?

Something more serious?

I know what kind of injuries these guys can sustain. And being the stubborn players they are, they play through them.

"Princess?"

Cash is at the door, Puck at his feet. He leans down to scratch behind Puck's ears, then stands back up with a smile on his face that's hard to see with the light behind him.

"Finally." I run to him but draw up short. "Are you okay?"

"I'm fine."

He turns and both of us follow Puck inside. Puck immediately goes to the new bone that is sitting on his bed in front of the fireplace. I follow Cash to the living room where he shrugs out of his jacket and undoes his shirt before sprawling on the couch.

"Cash, that was quite a hit. Are you sure?"

I sit next to him, wanting to run my hands all over him.

Highlights from tonight's game and the others are playing on a loop. Cash shifts, resting his head in my lap.

"I'm fine." There's a slight twist to his face as he says that.

"You would be more convincing if you didn't wince as you did that."

Cash glares up at me from his spot on the couch. "It's nothing."

"You don't have to put on a front for me."

He sighs, sinking into me. "It really fucking hurts."

"Can I see?"

Cash nods, pulling his shirt off. His ribs are taped, but it doesn't hide the purple and black marring his entire left side.

"Oh my God! How did you manage to play the rest of the night?" I go to touch it, but think better of it. I don't want to cause him any additional pain.

"It's what we do. Nothing was broken."

"Can I do anything for you?"

My eyes don't leave his side. I don't think I've ever seen a bruise that bad.

He closes his eyes, shaking his head. "I'll be okay."

"Cash." My voice is firm. "Let me help you. What do you need?"

"Did you have fun at the game with Angie?"

"Changing the subject, I see."

I stroke my fingers through his hair. His eyes close at my touch. I can see his eyelids fluttering as I brush through the silky strands.

With the low light from the TV, Cash looks soft. Beautiful even. I don't know how, but he takes my breath away.

"I told you, I'm fine."

"And you don't need anything. Got it."

I settle my other hand on his stomach, letting the warmth seep into me. If he wants to be stubborn, fine. But that doesn't mean I can't try and help him in my own way.

"Can I confess something?"

"Is it bad?" Cash asks, turning into my touch.

"I got nervous. Coming here tonight without you."

"Why?"

"I guess I'm still scarred from finding Duncan screwing Ava. Not that you were," I hurry to finish. "But I guess it did a little more trauma than I realized."

Cash's eyes open, a fierce expression on his face. "That

will never happen, Piper. Never. Fake relationship or not, I would never do that to you. Or any woman."

"I know." I squeeze the strands of his hair in my fist, letting him know I understand him. "It's just hard to not think that once it's happened."

"You deserved better than him."

"Someone like you?"

"Better than me."

Cash's eyes drift shut and I go back to rubbing his head. I want to tell him that there isn't a better man than him. I don't know if he would believe me.

He doesn't let people in, but I've seen the real him.

"I want your voice."

"You want to steal it like a wicked sea creature?" I laugh.

Cash peeks one eye open at me as I continue scraping my hand through his hair.

"No. Listening to you talk helps."

"Oh." I try not to blush. I don't think anyone has ever said anything like that to me before. "What do you want to hear about?"

"Anything. Nothing. You decide." He sighs. "Just don't stop."

I trace my fingers up and down his bare chest as I move my other hand to rub his temples. He leans into my touch.

"Test was good. Should know how I did in a few days, but I know I aced it."

Between the internship, Cash, and studying, it's hard to make time for much else. But I want to prove to people that I deserve my spot with my team. Even if my brother helped me get it.

"I knew you would. You're the smartest person I know, Princess."

"Not just a pretty face."

"Who told you that?" Cash's eyes fly open. They're staring at me, locked onto my own. "Was it that douchebag?"

I shrug a shoulder. "Yes. Friends. People see my blonde hair and big blue eyes and think there's nothing else to me."

"Really?"

I nod. It's not something I like to admit. There's the old adage about dumb blondes for a reason. "I try not to let it bother me, but sometimes it does. I think because of my dating history and the way I look, people think I just want to be a trophy wife."

Cash sits up, wincing as he spins around to pull me onto his lap. "People really think that?"

I nod but don't say anything. Maybe not being vulnerable with people makes them think I don't have much substance.

I don't want him to see all that, so I focus on his chest.

"Piper." Cash tips my chin up so I have to look at him. His eyes are blazing. "When I say you're one of the smartest people I know, I mean it. Sure, you're sexy as hell, but that's not the thing that makes me attracted to you."

"It's not?"

Cash laughs. "It's not a bad thing, but I've seen how you are with everyone around you. You're smart. And kind. And you make everyone around you feel like they are the most important person in the room. That's a hard quality to come by. And I would know."

"What do you mean?"

"I didn't get a lot of that growing up."

"You didn't?"

Cash never likes talking about his childhood. I've asked

him in the past, but he's brushed it off. This is the first time he's even hinted about it.

"I was good at hockey. When my dad realized that, that's all I became to him. A means to an end. If I was playing well, I was doing my job. But if I got into fights, I got attention."

"That's why you were always causing trouble on the ice."

He nods. "I'm not proud of it, but it was a hard pattern to break."

"Because you wanted your dad's attention."

"Yeah." He scrubs a hand over his face. This time, the pained expression isn't from his injury, but from cracking his chest wide open to me.

"What about your mom?"

"She cut out when I was three. Never saw her again."

"Cash."

He pulls me closer, hands drifting up and down my side. "I don't want your pity. From what I gleaned from my dad, she wasn't cut out to be a parent. Neither was he for that matter."

"Still. You shouldn't have had to fight for attention like that."

"It's the only thing I knew how to do."

"Do you still see him?" I ask.

He shakes his head. "He died when I was in college. But the need to impress him hasn't really left I guess."

"Oh Cash."

My heart aches for him. At the sweet little boy that was raised like that. It's the image he shows the world. The bad boy. The villain. Someone not to be messed with.

But that's not the real Cash.

It's the man sitting in front of me. Whose tender heart was battered and bruised growing up. Cash put up walls to protect himself. I can't blame him when that's how he grew up.

"Thank you." I press a kiss to his lips.

"For what?"

I rest my hand over his heart. "For telling me. I know it's not easy."

"I don't like people feeling sorry for me." He blows out a breath, cupping my cheek to pull me in closer. "Especially you."

"All I see is a person who survived the only way they knew how. I'm glad you told me."

"Only you, Princess. You're the only person I've told."

His words carry a weight I never would have imagined. This thing between us has an end date. I went into it with eyes wide open. Spending time with Cash to help him? I've done worse things.

But now that he's opening up to me? Telling me things he's never told anyone else?

I want to be worthy of this man's secrets. I want to be the person that he can continue to turn to when things don't go right in his life.

Can I? Can we keep this thing going? No wonder Cash doesn't do relationships. His mom left him and his dad only wanted him for his own gain.

"You're looking a little murderous there."

"I just hate that your parents were like that."

"It is what it is."

Cash's face has gone soft. Both of us are just looking at each other. Really seeing one another.

"It seems like we have more in common than we think."

"Not letting people in?" he asks.

"More like not letting ourselves be vulnerable with people."

"Being vulnerable with you is easy," Cash whispers against my lips. "Easier than I thought it would be."

"Your secrets are safe with me, Cash." I place a sweet kiss on his soft lips.

"I know." He brings me in closer and we sit like this for who knows how long. Soaking in each other's strength having bared our weaknesses to one another.

"I know this might be a big ask…" I say into his neck. It might be easier if I'm not looking at him.

"What?"

"Come over for Christmas dinner next week. I know you're gone on a road trip until then, but come for dinner with my family."

"What?" Cash pulls back, looking into my eyes. "You want me to come over for a holiday?"

"I know this thing is fake, but if you don't have plans, I want you to come with me. You and Puck."

Puck runs over to the couch and hops on when he hears his name.

"Are you sure? I'm not the type that people bring home to meet the parents."

"I wouldn't invite you if I didn't mean it. Assuming you don't have other plans."

"You really mean it?" I can hear the nerves in his voice. You wouldn't know it from the look of steel on his face.

"Yes."

"Then I guess I'm celebrating the holidays with the Fields family."

Chapter Sixteen

CASH

"We need to be on our best behavior tonight, Puck."

His tongue is lolling out of his mouth as he perches in the front seat of my truck. I clip his leash on before I give him one more scratch and get out of the car.

I'm nervous as I open the door and grab my purchases from the front seat. Not even before my first NHL game or the Stanley Cup finals was I this nervous.

Because I'm about to meet Piper's parents for dinner.

And not just any dinner…Christmas dinner.

I've never done this before in my entire life. I'm not someone you bring home to meet your mom and dad. I'm usually the one you sneak out at night to go meet.

Puck sniffs the grass as we walk to the front porch. My foot hits the wood as the front door swings open and Piper comes out.

She looks…well, I'm not sure what she looks like as she comes into the light of the porch.

"Uhh, Piper…what are you wearing?"

"This?" She pulls the sweater away from her. "Noah gave it to me as a joke. Didn't think I'd wear it."

The blue sweater is covered in patches with the Black Diamonds logo, lights sticking out from different places. It flashes in an array of colors, making it even uglier.

I groan. "Please don't show this to Cassie because she'll make me wear one."

Piper beams up at me. It tells me everything I need to know.

"There's one for me, isn't there?"

Piper nods. "Puck too."

"Your brother got my dog a sweater?"

"Uh-huh." Puck takes this opportunity to bark between the two of us. "I'm sorry, Puck. I didn't say hi to you."

Piper kneels down and plants a kiss on his muzzle. I blow out a breath, trying to shake out the nerves.

"You okay?" Piper asks, returning to her feet.

"Do you think your parents will like me?" I blurt out.

Wow, way to be cool, Cash.

"Why wouldn't they?" Piper asks.

"Maybe the fact that we're not really dating?"

"They don't know that though."

Cassie told us we have to make this thing believable. Spending the holidays? I don't think it gets more real than that.

Still. It does nothing to calm the nerves coursing through me.

"Will they like me though?" I ask again, staring up at the front of a brick, two-story house. Black shutters line the house. Two chairs sit in the corner of the porch. Everything about this place looks homey. Somewhere Piper would've grown up.

"Of course they will."

Her words do nothing to reassure me. Nothing about

my appearance gives people the warm fuzzies. Too many tattoos. Too much of a scowl. Dark eyes and a darker look to match.

"Cash. You are way overthinking this. Just act like you would when you've met your past girlfriends' parents."

"And how would that be?" I ask.

Piper gives me a quizzical stare. I try not to squirm under her intense gaze. I never knew a pair of blue eyes could be so intense.

"Have you never met a girlfriend's parents before?"

"Why is that so unbelievable?" I snap back. Too quickly.

A smile lights up Piper's face. She is enjoying this far too much for my liking. "Cash. I promise, just act like you do when you're around me."

So pretend not to think about her naked? Doesn't seem like sound advice, but something I can work with.

"I just hope your dad likes me."

Piper squeezes my arm one last time before opening the door. "It's not my dad you have to worry about."

Oh shit.

And here I was thinking that her dad would be the hardest person to win over.

I follow Piper inside, doing my best not to stare at her ass. The last thing I need is to have one of her parents see me checking her out.

The house feels smaller on the inside than I expected. An office sits off to the left with a smaller sitting room on the right.

"C'mon." Piper grabs my hand and doesn't let me linger in the entryway. She grabs Puck's leash from me as I kick off my shoes. The hallway is lined with pictures of their family. Of Noah playing hockey. Her dad playing football. What looks like family trips to the mountains. School pictures. Everyday things that make up a family.

Something I never had growing up.

The hallway opens up to a cozy living room, fire blazing in the fireplace with the Christmas tree decorated with haphazardly made ornaments, likely from when Piper and Noah were little. An oversized sofa and love seat dissect the room that flows into the kitchen beyond it. It's not anything that's overly modern.

It's well-loved. A sweet aroma fills the room from a candle flickering on the table.

It's then my eyes sweep over the couple sitting at the barstools at the counter. Noah is sitting next to them.

Here goes nothing.

"Mom. Dad." Piper drags me forward a few more feet. "This is Cash. My boyfriend."

"Still weird to hear that," Noah cuts in.

"Noah!" Piper seethes.

A woman with light blonde, bobbed hair rounds the counter and holds out her hand for me to shake. Piper is the spitting image of her. It's where Piper gets her beauty.

"Cash. It is so wonderful to meet you. I'm Tenley, Piper's mom. And this is her dad, Jackson."

"It's nice to meet you." I hand over the bouquet. "These are for you."

"That is so kind of you. Thank you."

I hold out my hand to shake her dad's hand.

"Cash." His voice is deep. Curt.

Piper said I didn't have to worry about her dad? That doesn't make any sense. He's intimidating as hell. He was a kicker in the NFL, so not like a giant lineman, but his presence is overwhelming, even though I'm taller than he is by a few inches. Gray peppers his hair.

"It's nice to meet you, sir." I hand over the bottle of bourbon. "This is for you."

Jackson takes it from me with a nod. "I appreciate that."

"Since when are you so formal?" Noah asks, popping a nut into his mouth.

"Noah." This time, from her mom. "We said you had to be nice tonight."

"What? It's not every day I get to see him act like an idiot."

"Noah!" All three of them yell at him this time.

"Is it too late to send Noah home?" Piper asks, grabbing a beer from the fridge for me.

"You mean you don't want to spend the holidays with your brother?" He wraps an arm around her and rubs his knuckles on her hair.

"Oh my God, stop!" she shrieks.

Tenley grabs the beer from Piper and hands it to me. "I'm sorry about them. I don't know where they get it."

"It's weird to see Noah like this, to be honest."

"Joys of being a big brother," she tells me. "Do you have any siblings, Cash?"

I shake my head, taking a sip of my beer. "It was just me growing up."

"Well, we're glad to have you here for dinner."

"Thanks for inviting me. And letting Puck come."

The dog in question has made himself at home, lying on his back in front of the fire. His favorite place to be.

"We couldn't let him be alone either." She squeezes my arm before going back into the kitchen. "Dinner should be ready soon."

Piper shoves Noah off her and walks over to me, calling over her shoulder, "I hope you get traded!"

"You wound me, Piper." He mocks being injured.

I can't help but smile at these two.

"It smells great in here."

"Piper made dessert," Noah tells me. "Her famous apple pie."

"What makes it famous?" I ask her as she comes up to me holding a matching sweater.

"If I told you, I'd have to kill you." She winks. "Now, c'mon. You need to put on your sweater before dinner."

It's then I notice everyone has one of the sweaters on. It makes my chest swell. Like I'm part of the family.

Piper leads me back through the hallway and up the stairs.

The hardwood floors creak beneath my feet. More pictures line the stairs.

"What's this picture?" I pull Piper to a stop.

It's her dad holding the Super Bowl trophy and a small baby.

"That was the night I was born." She rests her chin on my shoulder. "It's my favorite picture."

"You were born the night of the Super Bowl?" I ask, turning to look at her.

Piper nods. "Mom went into labor just before halftime. Dad made it just in time."

"Wow. That's quite the story."

There's another picture next to it. One of all of them together in matching T-shirts, with the trophy front and center. Piper and Noah are both screaming but I don't think I've ever seen two parents look happier.

Piper tugs my arm, moving me farther up the stairs. Everything about this place explains Piper. She grew up with more love than I ever experienced. It's a wonder some man hasn't snatched her up already.

Thank God they haven't because she's mine now.

For however long she'll have me.

The room Piper pulls me into has soft gray walls and a dark purple bedspread. Prints of flowers and mountains hang on the walls. It's Piper through and through.

"This is my room. You can change in here." She flops back onto the bed, eyes roving over me.

"Uh-uh. Don't look at me like that." I kick the door shut behind me. "No funny business, Princess."

"I'm not getting any ideas, Cash."

The way she says my name tells me she has all the ideas.

"Your parents are downstairs," I whisper. Grabbing the neck of my shirt, I pull it over my head and drop it next to her.

Piper's eyes trail over the bruise. It's gone down some, yellowing at the edges.

"It looks better."

"Feels better too."

"Good." Piper stands, resting her hands on my sides before pushing up on her tiptoes. "Do you have time for one kiss?"

"I can always spare a kiss for you, Princess."

Wrapping an arm around her waist, I dip her low. Shock covers her face as I smile right before laying one on her.

I love the way her fingers dig into my shoulders, holding on. I lick my way into her mouth, wanting more. No, demanding more.

We both get swept away in the heat of the kiss. I know I shouldn't, but I do. Until someone is calling out for us.

"Piper! Cash! Dinner is on the table!" a voice from downstairs calls out.

I pull back, staring down at Piper's wet lips. "Better get going."

"Don't forget to put your sweater on." She grins at me.

Piper helps me tug it over my head. "How do I look?"

She throws her head back in laughter. "You look way too hot to be wearing this."

"Good." I nip at her lip before dragging her downstairs. I don't want anyone to come looking for us.

By the time we get downstairs, Puck is already in his sweater, chewing on a bone.

"I hope you don't mind," Tenley tells me, setting a dish on the table, "but we got some bones for him."

I smile back at her. "Not at all. That's very kind of you. I'm surprised he's so happy. He usually doesn't like people."

She nods. "Piper told us. He didn't fight us when we put the sweater on. Gave him some treats."

"Looks like it worked."

We all take our seats around the table as dishes are passed around. They're chatting about everything and anything. It makes me feel like I'm a part of something, even if I'm not talking.

For once, the lonely feeling of spending the holidays by myself isn't there. Normally, I spend the day at the arena getting in a good, hard workout. Instead, I went for a walk with Puck before bringing him here.

The two of us spending the day like most people. With a family.

It's a feeling I don't want to get used to. Because Piper isn't mine to keep.

"How are you feeling after that hit?" Jackson asks.

I waggle my head, taking a heaping spoonful of green beans. "Not the worst hit I've ever taken."

"Do you think you'll be ready for the next game?"

"Nothing will stop him," Noah chimes in.

"Damn right, Strawberry."

"Strawberry?" Tenley asks.

Noah groans. "It's my nickname."

"Aww, my sweet strawberry." His mom claps him on the cheek. "How did I not know this?"

"I hate you, Willy," Noah tells me.

"Nah, you love me." I blow a kiss at him.

Conversation carries on around us as we eat the incredible meal Tenley cooked. Beef tenderloin. Garlic mashed potatoes. Green beans. I never would have had something like this on my own.

"I don't know if I'll be able to eat dessert," I groan, setting my napkin on my plate. "That was delicious."

"Thank you, Cash." Tenley smiles back at me.

"We can clear the table," Piper says.

"Actually, I'd like a word with Cash." Jackson tilts his head toward the hallway and I dutifully follow.

The room he goes into is one I haven't seen. It's full of dark wood and leather furniture. Pictures of him playing are on one wall with two gaudy rings sitting in the center of a dark wooden bookshelf.

His Super Bowl rings.

"Piper's been through a lot these last few months." Jackson's voice is very matter-of-fact as he pulls a bottle of bourbon and two tumblers out of a cabinet. "Her ex did not treat her well."

"He's a douche."

Jackson smirks at me, handing me a glass.

"I'm aware."

"Sorry. I know he's my teammate and all, but I can't stand him. Especially with how he treated Piper."

"And how do you feel my daughter should be treated?"

"Like the princess that she is." The words come out faster than I expect. I don't need to blow smoke up Piper's dad's ass, but it's true.

"Good."

"Duncan was a dick to her. I will never hurt her like that."

Not if I can help it. Even if I don't deserve Piper. Piper is goodness personified. She's sweet, kind, caring, and sexy as hell. I'm not even in the same league as her.

"You better not. Otherwise you will have the entire wrath of the Fields family coming down on you."

"The entire family, sir?"

He gives me an assessing glare, nodding his head. "Yes. We will do whatever it takes to protect her from getting hurt again."

I swallow down the last of my drink. It's always the quiet ones you have to be worried about.

"I understand. It is not my intention to hurt Piper."

Again with the assessing glare. This is why I never went home with any of my past girlfriends. If you can even call them that. It's not like I gave in to the bunny lifestyle of hockey, but I had the occasional steady woman that I kept around.

Too many issues to want to make things permanent with anyone.

"Good." Jackson swallows down the last of his drink before heading back to the kitchen. Not before stopping in front of me. "I like you, Cash. Don't let me down."

I smile into my drink. It felt like a test I had to pass tonight. Piper's family means everything to her. Even if this thing isn't real, I didn't want to be a dick to her family.

I guess she's rubbing off on me in more ways than I thought.

Dessert is already being tucked away into containers by the time I head out to the kitchen.

"We're going to head out," Piper tells me, smiling at me from the counter.

"What, no dessert? I want to try some of your famous apple pie."

"It'll keep." She bounds over to me. "I'm ready to go."

"Wait!" Piper's mom calls out. "I want a picture of you three before you go."

Piper rolls her eyes but walks over to the tree to get Puck situated. He would follow any command she gives him.

"You know what this means, right?" Noah asks from beside me.

"What?"

"Welcome to the family."

Chapter Seventeen

CASH

By the time we get home and get Puck situated with a bone, the need swirling between the two of us is palpable.

"That was the longest twenty minutes of my life," Piper tells me, walking backward up my stairs.

"You're telling me."

I race after her as she turns and darts up the stairs. I grab her, sweeping her over my shoulder as I step into my room and shut the door.

Throwing her onto the bed, I watch as Piper's eyes drink me in.

"Nothing but my mouth and cock are going to get you off tonight, Piper."

"I can't believe we've waited this long."

"Not because I haven't wanted to."

Fucking hockey schedule. If I could spend every night with her, I would. But I can't.

Piper crooks a finger at me, beckoning me forward. Pulling off my ugly sweater, I toss it on the floor. By the time I'm at the bed, I'm stark naked.

Piper sits up, dragging a finger along my cock.

"You want a taste?" I punch my hips toward her.

She shakes her head, looking up at me.

"What, seriously?"

"I don't like blow jobs."

"Really?"

"Your cock is huge. There's no way it wouldn't kill me if I tried to suck you off. No, thank you."

I smirk. "Doesn't orgasm mean little deaths in French?"

"Only if you come at my mouth with that thing."

I shouldn't be laughing, but I am. "Princess, you are one of a kind."

I lift her into my arms and move her farther up the bed. "You're not mad?"

"Mad that you don't like blow jobs?"

"Yeah."

"I'm not going to lie and say I don't wish I could feel you sucking me off, but I can't wait to be buried inside you."

"Then what are you waiting for?"

I crush my mouth to hers, heeding her words. Every pass of her tongue against mine sends heat straight to my cock.

Piper and I are clawing at each other. Needing to be skin on skin. She rocks into me, grinding down on my cock.

"So sweet." I lick my way into her mouth, not getting enough of her sweetness.

Short nails dig into my shoulders, pulling me closer. I swallow every gasp and moan that escapes. My hands skim over her sweater.

"Princess." I kiss my way down her jaw. "You're driving me crazy."

"More, Cash." Piper tilts her head to the side. "More."

I lick and suck my way down her neck. "How much more do you want?"

"All of you. I want all of you, Cash."

I nip at the tender skin of her neck. "You have me, Princess."

Piper pulls back, scraping her nails through the short stubble lining my jaw. "I like this. But you know what I'd like even more?"

"What?" I growl.

"I'd like it even more between my legs."

Piper's smile is sinful.

"Whatever you want, Princess."

I strip her sweater off, and her bare tits are exposed to me. Piper not wearing a bra does something to me. Seeing the immediate need she has for me in how tight her nipples are amps up my own pleasure.

Soft. Silky. Perfect.

Just like her.

"Piper." My voice is husky. "You are the sexiest woman on the planet."

I can only stare at her. Redness from my stubble coats her neck. Hair disheveled. Eyes needy. Lips swollen from our kisses.

"I have so many dirty thoughts on what I want to do to you."

I punctuate each word with a kiss down her neck until I reach her chest. Her tits are small but perky. I drag my tongue along one hard nipple.

"Keep doing that. I like that."

Piper is blissed out. Her blue eyes are closed, hands fisting in my navy sheets.

"Tell me more of what you want. What you like." I give the same attention to her other nipple. Taking it between my teeth, I lavish her with attention.

"I like it when you kiss me. And when I get eaten out."

"I can do that, Piper."

God, and now it is the only thing on my mind. Burying myself between her legs and drinking up every last drop of her sweet pussy.

Kissing my way down her soft stomach, I pop the button on her jeans and snick the zipper down. She's wearing a pair of purple underwear with a bow on the hem.

They are so perfectly Piper, I can't help but smile at her.

"What?" One eye is popped open at me.

I tug her jeans down her thighs, over her knees, past her calves and off, throwing them over my shoulder.

"These,"—I drag a finger along the hem—"look so sexy on you. A present just for me."

Piper is a squirming mess beneath me. I like that I make her this crazy. It's only fair, I suppose, since my dick is dying to get inside her.

"Take them off me," Piper whimpers.

"Not yet, Princess." I give her a cunning smile as I drag my nose over the material covering her pussy. "I haven't played with you enough."

Pushing her knees up and apart, I take in the wet spot on the satin of her underwear. I know—without a shadow of a doubt—that if I ripped these off her and sunk my finger inside her, she'd be dripping.

Piper is not one to hide how she feels. Every emotion plays out across her face. She shows me every time we're together what she's feeling.

She's not hiding that now. Not when she's bared open to me like this.

Something I could use a lesson in.

I don't show myself to anyone. But Piper? I wouldn't mind showing her more of myself.

But not right now. Right now, I need to put this woman out of her misery.

I bite on her hip. Nibble my away along her underwear to nip at the other side. Kiss my way down her thigh. I give her attention everywhere except where she really wants me.

"Don't make me take matters into my own hands, Cash Williams."

"Tsk, tsk. You've already done that. I'd have to punish you."

"Like smacking my ass?"

I growl. "You want that, Princess? Because I can give it to you."

"Do it, Cash. Make me come."

Gliding my hands up her body, I push her back onto the bed and pull her underwear off. Piper tracks my move as I shove my face into them like last time and take a deep breath. The musky scent sends fire rolling through me. One strike of a match and I'd be a goner.

"Do you know that the way your pussy smells drives me mad? So fucking good."

Right now, all my focus is on the woman laid out before me. Because she needs to come on my tongue before I let her come on my dick.

"Lie back, center of the bed." Piper scoots her way up the bed, spreading her legs wide for me. "Is that what you want, Princess?"

"Yes."

I crawl up the bed like an animal stalking his prey. I take the invitation, burying my face between her legs.

"Cash!" Piper screams, sinking her fingers into my hair.

She pulls tight and it has me pushing my dick into the sheets of my bed.

I'm a starving man. Ravenous as I eat her out with a fury I've never felt. I can't get enough. Her sweet juice runs down my chin as I attack her pussy and her clit. Doing everything I can to get her to come.

"C'mon, Princess. Let me feel you come on my tongue."

I push my tongue inside, flicking it. Curling it.

With that, it tips Piper over the edge as she comes undone.

I smile against her as I suck down every last drop. I pop up, wiping my mouth as she's splayed out below me. Moving over her, I press a kiss to the corner of her mouth.

"You think you can do that again?"

"For you? Yes."

Piper takes my mouth in a hot, hungry kiss. I'm rocking against her as she tastes her release on me.

Strong thighs wrap around my waist, holding me close.

"Fuck." I manage to tear my lips away and stare down at the wet heat my cock is sliding through. "You're going to make me come like this if you aren't careful."

Piper pushes me back and sits up, dragging a finger along my dick.

"I can't wait to feel all of these inside me." Her fingers trace each piercing on my cock. She's studying it, like she's trying to memorize it.

"You don't have to keep staring at it."

Piper drops a kiss on the swollen head and lies back on the bed. I throw my head back in pain. "You tease."

"No teasing. I'm ready for you, Cash."

"I know we talked about this, but do you want to use condoms?"

It was more a heat-of-the-moment conversation when

she was getting off, but if we don't have to, I don't want a single damn thing between the two of us.

"No. I want to feel all of this inside me without anything between us. But…"

"But what?" I kiss her again. I can't help myself.

"I want to ride you."

I smile against her and flip us over. "Do it."

Piper shifts, grabbing my hard length and sinking down. Inch by slow inch. "Holy shit."

She stills halfway down.

"You okay?" I reach forward, rubbing the pad of my thumb over her clit. Helping ease her down over me.

"I've never felt anything like it."

It takes everything in me not to rock up and sink myself inside her. I want her to take this at her own pace.

"Cash, I need you to…"

"Need me to what?"

"To fuck me."

Sweeter words have never been spoken.

"How, Princess? Tell me and I'll do it."

Piper slips off me and lies face down on the bed, pushing her ass in the air. I don't waste any time, shuffling in behind her and dragging my slick cock through her ass crack.

"Fuck, Piper." I squeeze her ass cheeks together, loving the feel of her bare skin. My hands have a mind of their own, brushing over all that skin exposed to me. "You'd look so good with my handprint here."

"Do it, Cash."

A loud, resounding crack echoes through the bedroom as I slap her ass.

"Gah!"

"That's my girl." I do it again. The red blooming there has my cock twitching. "All mine, Princess."

"Make me yours."

"Fuuuuck." I don't waste another minute, pushing inside her. Her tight heat chokes me to within an inch of my life.

"This is my favorite place to be. Buried deep inside you."

Piper wiggles her hips, driving me ever crazier.

"You feel incredible." Her voice is full of lust. Desire.

I piston my hips inside of her, setting an easy pace. Feeling each drag inside her and how amazing it feels.

"I won't break, Cash. Harder."

I pull Piper up to my chest, my hand creeping up to tweak her nipples as I continue driving inside of her.

Harder.

Faster.

Deeper.

Every gasp and moan drives me wild.

"Are you going to come on my cock for me?"

"Yes," she whispers. "Oh God, yes."

"Then do it."

I bite down on the tender skin of her neck and she explodes.

"Fuck! Fuck, fuck, fuck!" I jack my hips once, twice, and explode inside of her. "Holy shit!"

Piper wraps her hands around my own, keeping me close. I lower us to the bed, not able to withstand keeping us upright.

I slip out of her, watching as my cum drips out of her.

"You look so good. Marked by me, Princess."

Piper melts in my arms.

"My Prince Charming."

Chapter Eighteen

CASH

PRINCESS

Are you ready for the game tomorrow?

CASH

I hope. I'm ready to crush Nashville

Is it bad I say I want you to do the same?

No. I like it

Why are they the worst team in hockey?

Because they're dicks

Do you think you'll be able to call me after the game? I miss you

I miss you too, Princess. I wish I were at home in bed with you

Yeah? What would you be doing to me?

Fuck. You realize I'm in a hotel room with my teammate, right?

And I'm not. I'm horny and wish my boyfriend were here with me.

Fuuuuuuck. I wish I was there and could eat that pretty little cunt of yours

I miss your tongue. The things you do to me. Your pierced cock

You realize how hard you're making me?

How hard?

Want me to show you?

Yes

<<picture of dick here>>

I wish I was there and could feel that inside me

I wish I was too, Princess. You know how I love being inside of you and making you crazy

If only I could travel with the team. My problem would be a lot easier to solve

What problem? I want pictures

<<topless picture here>>

You know how I love those tits of yours. I wish I was fucking them right now

You always play great after we spend the night together

It's a theory I wish I never had to put to the test by being apart

> I wish you were here

> I do too. But I have to go. I need a cold shower if I have any hope of sleeping tonight

> I guess I'll just have to get myself off

> Princess. You can't tell me that and then leave

> ...

> Just you wait. When I get home, I'm going to fuck you senseless

> I can't wait <3

"Fuck yeah!" I slap Troy on the helmet as I skate to him after another amazing goal. We've been dominating this game against Nashville so far.

After getting our asses handed to us at the beginning of the season, it's nice to know we can rally against a conference rival.

"Great teamwork, guys!" Troy butts heads with one of the defenders who cleared the way for him to score. "Let's keep doing that and we've got this game in the bag."

I skate back to the bench as the second string comes out. The Nashville crowd is booing us. It makes me want to flip them all off, but I don't. I think of Cassie and how she would react to that.

We're currently up 4-1 in the third period. The last time we played the Knights, we got crushed. Tonight, it's almost easy.

No win ever is. But tonight's game is fun. The team is

working as one. Offense. Defense. Every person is working together in a way I haven't seen in a while.

The rest of the game goes by in a blur of boos and goals. Colorado pulls out an easy win, 6-2. We line up to shake hands with them before heading to our locker room. By the time we get into the visiting team's locker room, the press are waiting for us.

We don't have a minute to breathe before they descend.

"Cash, how do you feel about this team win?" The reporter shoves his mic in my face. Guys all over the locker room are talking to the various reporters. The locker room is as bare bones as you can get. Every visiting locker room is this way.

Hard metal benches. Basic lockers. No frills. They do it to psych you out. They don't want to replicate the coziness of your own locker room. The more you settle in, the easier it is for you to get an edge on the home team.

"I don't know if you saw how well our captain was playing, but he dominated the ice tonight. It's lucky I get to be on the same team as him."

"Troy Hollins has made quite the name for himself these first few years in the league. What's it like playing with him?"

This kind of question would have annoyed me in the past. Not tonight. Tonight? Tonight, I'm smiling thinking of Piper and how I would answer this question if she were the one asking me.

"He's a great teammate. Someone who is always learning and always teaching you more about the game. Troy is the kind of player who elevates your own game so you're not disappointing him."

The reporter is practically beaming at me. I wish I could

snap a picture and send it to Cassie to tell her how well I'm doing. But I can't. Instead, I smile back at him as he moves on down the row of lockers to talk to Strawberry about his play.

I make quick work of my shower and changing because the last thing I want is to hang around here. There's an itchiness to me tonight. I had two goals and two assists tonight. It was one of my best games. The one person I want to share it with isn't here.

I grab my bag before heading out to the tunnel to get on the bus.

"Cash, wait up!"

I recognize the voice as they close the distance between us.

"Cassie. How are you?"

Cassie comes to a dead stop, a look of shock on her face. Cassie doesn't come to every away game, but on these long stretches, she pops in every now and then.

"I don't think you've ever asked me how I was doing before."

"Get outta here. Of course I have."

"You haven't. And I have to say, if this is Piper's doing, I'm okay with it."

I roll my eyes before walking down the tunnel to the bus. We'll be staying here tonight in Nashville before leaving for New Jersey tomorrow.

"What can I say? I'm a changed man."

Cassie doesn't know what to do with herself. "I just ran into Weber and he gave me a preview of tomorrow's article. He is positively shitting rainbows about you."

"No he's not."

There's not a chance in hell that he is that effusive about me.

"Would you like me to tell you what he said?" Cassie

quirks a perfectly manicured brow at me. I have a feeling whether I say yes or no, she's going to do it regardless.

"Might as well since it seems like you want to."

She's beaming at me. "He said you had one of your best games, statistically speaking, and how you passed off all the praise onto your teammates. Even said that Troy is the kind of player who elevates your own game so you don't disappoint him. Said how far we're going to go with you at the helm."

"Shit. He said that?"

No one has ever been that nice about me. Especially a reporter that I have been an asshole to. I realize that now. Well, Piper helped me realize that.

"I don't know what Piper has done for you, but keep it up, Cash. The press are loving you and it's making my life easy."

I give Cassie my easiest smile. "For you, Cassie? I'll do whatever you need me to do. Give yourself a pat on the back."

"Does that mean you think I was right? I never thought I would see the day."

"Clearly it's not going to your head."

"Ahh, there's the Cash I know and love."

"I'm not all that reformed."

She shakes her head, giving my bicep a squeeze. "I never would've believed that in the past, but now I do. So keep it up. The less I have to deal with you, the better."

She leaves in a haze of perfume and know-it-allness. If it were anyone else, I'd call them out. But Cassie isn't wrong. Piper has completely helped transform my image after being with her for only a short time.

I wish I could say she was wrong when she decided to put this plan together, but she wasn't.

"Nice to see you too, Cassie!" I call out after her, but she's gone.

I head onto the team bus where most of the guys are waiting.

"Willy. Want to hit the town tonight?" one of the guys asks from the seat behind me.

"Nah, I'm good."

"Seriously? We always thought you'd be down for a good time."

"I want to talk to Piper tonight."

"Damn. You're whipped."

"Don't I know it," I agree with a laugh.

Because it's true. I never was one to turn down going out with the team. It always helped prevent me from going home on my own.

I used to love long road trips. Being in a new city and a new hotel meant I wasn't at home by myself. Now I wish I were going home to Piper. At least at the end of this road trip, I'll be seeing her in Edmonton.

Now? Now I'm going to some cold, box-hotel room so I can talk to her. I haven't seen her in a few days, only exchanged a few texts with her here and there.

After that last one, all I want is to have some alone time with her. Whether it's in my hotel bathroom or a bar, I want some time with Piper.

Imagining her getting herself off has been the only thought I fall asleep to. That warm body of hers. The way she takes my cock. How she responds to me as she comes.

I never thought all of that was wrapped up in my Princess. But God, what a dirty little Princess she is. It's my life's mission to bring out the dirty side in her.

Piper Fields is the epitome of the best person there is. She'll do anything to help those around her. And seeing the dirty side come out during sex? I fucking love it.

Because that woman makes me crazy.

She's my first thought in the morning and my last thought in the evening. I have never been so concerned with another person in my life. But I am with Piper.

She's my person. I never thought I'd actually find one. But I have now.

The bus pulls up to the parking lot of our hotel and everyone gets off. Half the guys head toward one of the local bars while the others head to their rooms.

I'm thankful my roommate is still of the partying kind. It means I'll have my room to myself.

I wave a few goodbyes to teammates as we head into the elevators and make our way to our rooms. Everything about this hotel is standard. Posters of the city line the beige walls. Worn down, patterned carpets rest on the floors.

I waste no time stripping out of my suit down to only my boxers, hanging up the jacket and pants then crashing onto my bed.

We've done nothing but traverse the country the last week, and it's hard to know what time zone I'm in. Getting comfy in the bed, I immediately video call Piper.

She answers on the second ring.

"There's my stud of a player." A sleepy smile sits on her face.

"Hey Princess."

Even though we played in Nashville, an hour ahead of Denver, the game still ended late. Piper looks exhausted. I wish I could scoop her up into my arms and fall asleep with her.

Fuck. When did I become this man that didn't *just* want to have sex with someone? Not that the sex with Piper isn't incredible.

Because it is.

But ask me a few weeks ago and I never would've wanted to *just* sleep with someone. Piper has completely changed the game.

"I am so proud of you, Cash."

I can't help the blush as I settle into bed.

"I wanted to do good just for you."

She shakes her head, tucking both hands under her pillow. "You don't need to perform for me. I can't believe that you beat Nashville like that."

"Oh no. I want you to be proud to be attached to me."

Piper scoots closer to the phone. I hate that we can only video chat while I'm away. It feels like I'll be away from her for months, even though it's not that long.

"Cash. You know how much I adore being with you. You never have to doubt that."

"Yeah?"

"Never." Piper's words are firm. "Whether this is fake or not, you are an incredible player and man. You deserve someone who is going to show you off. And that's me. I'll never not sing your praises."

God. What did I do to deserve this woman? From the very first meeting, I was the biggest dick to her. But then with one chance encounter with her ex, this thing between the two of us went from pretend to real.

I don't know if I'll ever get enough of Piper. Of her goodness. The sweetness that she shows everyone on a daily basis. I've never been ashamed to be with her, and she's never acted like she is ashamed of me.

It's something that I'm not used to.

"I wish you were here with me, Princess."

"After last night, I do too."

Last night. When she texted me how great I always played after we spent the night together.

"You know, we could put your theory to the test." I rest

my arm behind my head as my dick chubs beneath my boxers.

"Oh yeah?" Piper's eyes widen. If there's anything I've learned about her in the last few weeks, it's that her eyes give away everything. "What do you want to do?"

I rest my phone on my chest and shove my free hand in my boxers. "I want to see your tits."

"Tits for your dick." Piper is firm in her tone.

"What the Princess wants, the Princess gets."

I turn the view on my video call as I watch Piper take her top off. Those perfect tits of hers that I love so much fill the camera.

"Fuck me, Piper."

"I wish, Cash."

My cock fills her screen as I give myself a lazy stroke. "Do you know how much I hate being away from you now? How I wish I could spend every night in bed with you?"

"About as much as I do. I miss you, Cash."

Piper's eyes are soft as she tells me those words. I've never missed anyone in my life. No one ever missed me, so why would I miss them?

But Piper? I miss her. She's woven her way inside me in ways I can't even begin to tell people. She's the best person I know, and I don't know how she's in this with me.

"Touch yourself, Piper." It's the only thing I can do to break the hold on the emotions I have. I don't want to tell her what she means to me over a video chat. I want to do that in person. "I want you to finger yourself and tell me what you taste like."

"Cash," she moans before turning the view on her camera as she pushes two fingers inside of herself.

"Fuck, Princess."

I jack myself off as I listen to her get herself off. Her

hips are arching off the bed as her moans fill my ears. I couldn't care less if my roommate chose to come back at this time. Except no one gets Piper like this.

Only me.

I'm the only one that gets to see how much she wants me.

"I'm close, Cash."

"That's it, Princess. Get yourself off."

My hand moves faster as I get closer. Fuck. Watching the way she is on camera—she's giving me everything.

I want to give Piper everything. She deserves it.

"Cash!" Her voice screams over the phone as she comes and I erupt. I coat my hand and stomach, unleashing ropes of cum as we orgasm together over the phone.

"You are so fucking sexy, Princess. Look at you, all strung out for me."

"Only for you, Cash. No one else has ever made me feel this way."

Those words have something I can't put a name to blossoming in my chest.

Pride?

Lust?

Love?

I've never felt anything like this as I come down from my high. Grabbing my T-shirt from the foot of my bed, I clean myself up.

"Piper. I wish you were here with me right now. I want you in my arms."

"It's the only place I want to be, Cash. With you."

"I'll be home soon enough."

"I hate road games. Can I say that?"

I nod. "Yes."

Piper shifts in bed, turning over so her face fills the screen. "I'll be seeing you in Edmonton soon enough."

"And you'll finally be in my arms."

"Go get some sleep, Cash. I want you well rested for your next game."

I smile at her. Only Piper will cut things short so I can play better. I don't know what I did to deserve this woman, but I want to earn her.

"Night, Princess. Sleep well."

"Night, Cash."

I want to tell her so much more, but I don't. I let her go. Maybe I'll work up the nerves to tell her when I get home.

That I want more. That I want Piper.

"Have you ever been here?"

Piper links her fingers with mine as we stroll down the quiet street.

"Not to Edmonton."

"I never know where you've been."

She smiles up at me. Her cheeks are pink from the cold.

"Duncan never took me anywhere if that's what you're asking. And I'm a lowly intern. I don't travel with the team."

"I'm glad you get to come as my girlfriend. I've missed you."

Even if it's fake. Because Cassie said this would be a great opportunity to show everyone our relationship ahead of the stadium series.

We're on the last game of a six-game road trip. I'm excited that we get to play outdoors this week. Even more excited that Piper is here to experience it.

"Good excuse to travel, I guess."

"If you could go anywhere in the world, where would you go?" I ask.

"Hawaii."

"Really? I thought it'd be Paris."

Piper laughs. "Think you've got me pegged, Williams?"

"Apparently not."

"I love the sunshine. I want to lie on the beach with a coconut in hand and listen to the waves."

It puts the thought of Piper in a skimpy bikini on the beach into my head. Or rather, peeling her out of it.

"You know that's not fair to put that image in my head, right?"

"What, when it's all cold and snowy here?" Piper pulls her purple hat farther down her head. The ends of her hair curl out over her shoulders. She isn't wearing much makeup, but she's glowing.

It's something I'm starting to learn about her. I never really understood inner beauty before. But it radiates from Piper. It makes her one of the most beautiful people I know.

She's turning me into a sap.

"Are you going to imagine being on that beach tomorrow during the game?"

The weather changed and a snow storm is expected to blow through the city tonight. Nothing like playing hockey outside in the elements.

I haven't done it since I was in high school. I've always loved skating on a pond with the snow coming down.

I wish every game could be like that. Instead, now it's always under the lights and to the shouts of the fans.

"I'm going to have to if I want to survive."

"Okay." I laugh. "It's not going to be that cold."

"Will you warm me up after?" Piper shoves her hands under my jacket.

"Jesus! You're like ice!" I try to shake her off, but she holds on even tighter.

"See? I'm not going to make it through the game."

I pull her close, pulling her hat down lower. "Then I'm going to have to get you all the cold weather gear I can to keep you warm."

"I'll be the lunatic decked out in a marshmallow suit tomorrow trying to stay warm while cheering for Cash the Sex God."

"Cassie would kill you if you said that." I laugh.

"People have a right to know about their star defenseman."

"Will a kiss get you to keep quiet?" I whisper against her cold lips. "Keep you warm perhaps?"

"Yes and yes."

"Mmm." The kiss is sweet, soft. Mindful that we're in public, I don't give her everything I want.

Everything she deserves.

"C'mon, Cash. We need to get you fed before your skate this afternoon."

The team loosened the reins on restrictions since it's the first time they're playing in the stadium series. With the All-Star break fast approaching, I know all the guys are happy even for a few hours of peace.

"Cash Williams!" A little boy and his parents are standing at the corner we walk up to. "You're my favorite player!"

He's wearing a Black Diamonds knit hat and a coat that looks too big for him.

"I am?" I kneel down to get on his level. "Are you from Colorado?"

He shakes his head. "No. But you're the best! You're so fast on the ice."

I laugh. "You think so?"

He nods again. "Super fast!"

"Are you going to the game tomorrow?"

"Yes. Mommy and Daddy got us tickets."

"Make sure you cheer really loud for us then."

He nods. "I will! Can I get your autograph?"

"Sure thing. How about a picture too?"

"You don't mind?" his mom asks.

I shake my head. "Not at all. What's your name?"

"Austin."

"Austin." I grab a pen that Piper is holding out and sign the piece of paper that his mom hands me. "I'm glad I got to meet you."

"Me too. None of my friends will believe me."

His mom pulls out her phone and snaps a picture of the two of us.

"Make sure you show them that picture." I give him a high five.

"We'll tag you in it so the team can share it," his mom tells me. "I can't thank you enough. You're his favorite player."

"I appreciate it. Thank you."

They wave goodbye as I turn to Piper. She's beaming.

"What?" I wrap an arm around her shoulders and steer us across the street.

"That was the cutest thing I've ever seen."

"Stop it." I try to hide my smile but I can't. "It's nothing."

"I get why you like kids."

"No criticism." I boop her on the nose.

"You could just see how excited he was." Piper stops and pulls us out of the way of people on the sidewalk. A light snow has started to fall. "You made his day."

I shrug a shoulder. "It's what anyone would have done."

"Nope." She shakes her head. "Not everyone would have done that. You are incredible."

"I couldn't have ignored him. He was too excited."

"You were so cute with him."

Piper grabs the sides of my coat and hauls me into her. I tower over her. The streetlights flicker in her eyes. I don't know if it's the lights or her happiness sparkling there.

But it's a sight that hasn't gotten old.

Piper is nothing but pure goodness. I thought for sure I'd get sick of it. I've never been surrounded by someone like her, who is kind for no other reason than she wants to be that way.

Everyone in my life always had an ulterior motive. My dad beat that into my head, when it was really him that was always out for something.

"Have I told you how cute *you* are, Princess?"

She thinks for a second. "Not today."

I drop my forehead to hers. "My apologies, then. How could one minute have gone by without me telling you how fucking sexy you are?"

"I thought you were going with cute?"

I steal a quick kiss. "Cute. Sexy. Fucking gorgeous as hell."

This time, the kiss is longer. Slower. Piper presses up onto her toes, deepening it. My hands slide around her waist, pulling her close.

I love the way she slots against me. Every part of her fits into me. Like she was made for me. I get lost in her taste. In her feel. The way she smells.

I get lost in everything that is Piper.

Until she's pulling away, staring up at me with kiss-swollen lips.

"I don't think we can keep doing this here." She's biting down on her bottom lip.

"Fuck." I tug it from her clutches. "You drive me crazy."

I wish I didn't have the game tomorrow. I want to take Piper back to my hotel room and fucking ravish her.

I thought a few times with her would cure my need for her.

What an idiot.

All it's done is made me want her more. Crave her with a need I've never had before.

Piper, the sweet little Princess, falling for me, the villain.

"We should probably get to lunch."

"I forgot that's why we were out."

Because Piper steals all rational thought from my head.

And I wouldn't have it any other way.

Chapter Twenty

CASH

"Piper, you couldn't get your brother out?"

"Said he was too sore. "

"That was a gnarly hit he took," Nick tells us. He's on his own tonight. I guess he usually is, not that I know much about his life.

I haven't been the best at getting to know my team-mates over the years. Closed off was my mantra. Until Piper. She's changing everything about me for the better.

"He should've wanted to celebrate the win," one of the guys says.

I'm not paying that much attention. Piper's hand is on my leg, drawing small circles on the inside of my thigh. Making me crazy.

"Cash, you played great tonight," Piper tells me, leaning into my side.

I wrap an arm around her, keeping her there. The only place I want her.

"You think so?" I ask her, twirling a lock of hair around my finger. A few of the guys came out to celebrate our big win against Edmonton. They're one of the top teams in the league every year, and our rivalry with them is one for the ages.

Getting to win in a flurry of snow and goals?

It doesn't get much better than that.

"A goal and an assist? You were on fire."

Listening to Piper give me my stats is making me hard. Thank God we're in a dark club and no one can see us.

The second we arrived, we were escorted into the VIP section. One of the perks of being a professional athlete.

Piper left her jersey in my car, stripping down to her tank and jeans. It's nothing fancy, but she looks good. She always looks good.

"I'm surprised Cassie let me come out tonight."

"With me and the team? Good publicity. Even I know that."

Piper sips on her drink, and just watching that makes me crazy. Every single thing this woman does elicits a reaction. I don't know when I became so far gone for Piper, but I am. With the All-Star Game next month, we're racing toward the finish line of this thing between us. And I have no idea how I'm going to tell Piper I want more.

Does she want more? This isn't something I've ever had to do. Telling someone my feelings? I might as well try and solve world peace.

I only hope she feels the same way.

"I'm going to hit the bathroom."

Piper presses a kiss to my cheek before leaving my side.

I am shameless in watching her walk away. There's a slight sashay to her hips. As if she knows I'm going to watch. A smirk plays on my lips as she disappears down the hallway with a small turn back and a wink at me.

Oh, it's on.

"You okay, man?" someone asks from next to me. I

don't know who. Nick, maybe? I couldn't care less. Because the only thing on my mind is Piper.

And needing to make her mine.

I swallow down the rest of my drink and stand. "Gotta hit the bathroom."

PIPER

I'M HOPING Cash takes the hint. I'm a live wire ready to spark. Watching Cash play tonight got me, well, horny. There's something about the way he plays that captures my attention. His stick-handling skills? Next level. The way he can read the other team and make a play? He's one of the best in the league.

I'm only hoping he read my hint. Because I need him right now.

"Piper." His growl comes from down the hall as he stalks toward me. There's a gleam in his eyes. One that says he's going to devour me.

Grabbing my hand, he sticks his head inside the door to one of the bathrooms before pulling me inside and flipping the lock shut.

Warm lips crash down on mine the second my back hits the door. I grapple for purchase, needing to hold on to something.

"What are you doing to me?" Cash bites down on my lip, licking the sting away.

"Me? Do you know how hot watching you play makes me?"

Cash hoists me into his arms and presses his hard length between my legs.

"I'm dying, Piper. I need to be buried inside you." His lips nibble a path down my neck to my bare collarbone. I pulled off his jersey on the way over and went with jeans and a small black camisole. His hands are drifting up the material, pulling it down over my breasts. His hands tweak my nipples the way I love. I've never been well endowed, but Cash doesn't care. He loves my chest and lavishes it with attention. But right now, that's not where I want it.

Fisting my hands in his hair, I pull his face level to mine.

"What's stopping you? Fuck me, Cash."

It's the words I know he loves to hear.

An animalistic sound escapes his lips as he sets me on my feet and takes a step back. His dick is hard in his jeans.

I lick my lips, staring at him in his tight black tee. The dark blue lights of the bathroom make him look dangerous. Except I know the real Cash. And I've never felt safer.

Music booms loud outside the door, matching the beat of my heart.

"Take it out."

I take heed of his words. Rubbing my palm over his bulging erection, I pop open the button of his jeans and pull down the zipper. My gaze doesn't stray from his. His eyes are dark, full of a fire and the same lust that is coursing through me. Shoving the material open, I pull out his long, hard dick. I give it a slow stroke.

"Keep doing that," Cash tells me before pulling me in for another bruising kiss.

His tongue invades my mouth. It has me rubbing my legs together. I need the friction. Need something to quell the desire that's threatening to burst out of me.

"Do you know how sweet you taste? This fucking bourbon of yours."

He's drinking me in. Sipping on my tongue. Taking everything I'm giving him.

I'm dizzy with lust. The way his mouth claims mine is tipping me toward the edge.

"Now, Cash. I can't take it anymore."

Cash spins me and put my hands on the sink. Graffiti paints the walls. Colors bursting and mixing together. Our eyes lock in the mirror as he undoes my jeans and shoves them down my thighs. My breasts are hanging out of my cami. I look ravaged. Utterly destroyed by the man who I am falling for.

Cash steps in behind me, sliding his dick through my ass cheeks.

"Do you know how fucking hot you are? What you do to me?" Strong hands drift up my chest as he pulls me back against him.

I press my bare ass into him, urging him on.

"I think I know."

Cash slips between my legs, pistoning his hips forward. The pierced head comes into view.

"Hands on the sink, Princess."

I do as he says before he slams inside me.

"Cash!" I scream. I don't even try to keep my voice down. Not a soul could hear over the music, even if they had their ear pressed up against the door.

His hand snakes into my hair and pulls my gaze to his. Not that I could look away if I tried.

Cash sets a grueling pace. Every drag of those piercings inside me amps me up.

The pressure builds. My skin feels too tight.

"You're so good at taking my cock, Princess. The way you let me fuck you. Perfect. Absolutely perfect."

It's his words that send me barreling over the cliff. The

colors of the bathroom explode behind my eyes as I come. And come. Shooting off like a rocket into the stars.

Cash doesn't let up as he keeps going before he stills.

I don't know if I'll ever get used to the feeling of him bare inside me. The way it feels to have him fill me up with his cum.

I want it every day. Every day I can have him.

"Cash."

He presses a kiss to my neck, slipping out of me.

Cash's hands are tender as he puts me back together, pulling my underwear and jeans back up before tucking himself away.

My focus comes back down to earth. I look well fucked. There's no other way to describe it.

Cash wraps his arms around my waist and holds me. His eyes stay on me.

Like this, together, we fit. I don't see the bad guy he says he is. I don't see the princess he claims I am.

We're Cash and Piper.

The man I'm falling for and want to be with. For longer than the time we've been given. I want it to stay this way.

"I'm glad you came," he whispers.

"Me too." I turn, resting my ass against the sink. "You looked great out there. If you don't make it to the All-Star Game, you've been robbed."

"We'll see."

"I'll campaign on your behalf."

Cash laughs. "Calm down, Princess. If I don't make it, it's just a week I get to spend with you."

"A full week of just us? Maybe I should campaign they don't invite you."

Cash leans down to kiss me. "You're so easy to read."

"I just want you."

Only him.

Only Cash.

Just…him.

He's burrowed his way inside me and I don't know how I'm supposed to let him go in a few weeks' time.

"We better get back out there." One last kiss before he's peeking his head out into the hall. "Coast is clear."

Thank God for the privacy of the VIP section. I don't care if anyone would have seen us, but we have to be cautious about Cash's image. Even if he's had glowing articles written about him in the paper.

I don't think Cassie would approve of a sex scandal.

Right now, none of that matters.

Cash is what matters most.

Only Cash.

Chapter Twenty-One

CASH

"Cash. Do you have a minute?" Coach Barney asks as I skate off the ice.

"Sure." I grab my water bottle and take a healthy swig. With the All-Star Game coming up, the coaches are pushing us harder in practice.

Like they think we'll forget how to play hockey over a well-deserved break.

"I've got some good news for you."

"Yeah?"

A rare smile stretches out across his face. "Looks like you're coming with me to Nashville."

His words settle over me as I understand their meaning. For once, guys want to go play in Music City.

"I made the All-Star team?"

Coach Barney claps me on the shoulder. "You, Troy, and Duncan."

"Duncan?"

I can't imagine the Douche making the All-Star team, but as much as I hate to admit it, he's a good player. Self-ish, but good.

Coach ignores my question. "I'm proud of you, Cash. You've come a long way this season."

"I have?"

He nods. "You've always been a great player, one of the best I've coached. But something has changed in you this season. You're lighter. Happier. I don't want to see that go away."

"Thanks, Coach. I appreciate that."

"Now get outta here. The team will make all the arrangements for travel."

"You got it."

The rest of the guys are already off the ice, and I take a minute. Breathing all of it in. I do a lap around the rink before the Zamboni comes out to clean the ice. My skates grind into the roughed-up surface. It's familiar. A comforting sound.

Even in my best season before this one, I didn't make the All-Star team. I used it as an excuse to lie on a beach somewhere warm for the week.

It felt like a big middle finger to my dad that I didn't make it. That I was playing in the league but didn't make the elite—something he always wanted. No matter how high I reached, it was never high enough for him.

Now? Now I feel like I owe it all to Piper. The one person I can't wait to share my news with.

Skating off the ice, I go to find Piper.

"Hey."

I'm shocked to find her walking down the tunnel to me.

"Hi. What are you doing here?"

"Troy said you had some good news to tell me so I came to find you."

I sweep Piper up into my arms, wrapping her legs around my waist. "I got into the All-Star Game!"

"What!" Piper screeches. "Cash! That's amazing!"

Her hands come down on my cheeks as she lays one on me. I can feel her happiness flowing between the two of us.

This. This is why I wanted to tell her.

Fuck the deadline that Cassie gave the two of us. I know everything I've told Piper is that I'd rather be alone. But when the two of us get back to Denver, I want to make this thing permanent.

I don't know how I could ever let the woman in my arms go.

"Do you have to get back to practice?" she mutters against my lips.

"No."

"Good. You obviously know everything about being a hockey player since you made the All-Star team."

"Nothing left to learn."

"So you can stay here and kiss me."

We go back to kissing. I don't care that we're in the middle of the hallway. This is a moment I don't ever think I'll forget.

"I should go clean up," I whisper to her, holding her against the wall now.

"Ugh. Fine." She throws her arms around my neck, pouting. "Ignore your girlfriend wanting to celebrate your amazing news with you."

I nip at her lips. "The way I want to celebrate would not be appropriate here."

"Would you two get a room?"

I groan at hearing his voice. I guess it means we're really selling this if Duncan is complaining about us. Not that I care what he thinks. He's a dick, but I don't want him to see Piper like this.

Only me. Only I get to see her blissed out just from kissing.

"Grow up, Duncan," Piper tells him, sliding out of my arms.

"What, jealous you can't get a girl?" I put Piper behind me.

How much longer are we going to have to deal with this douche in our lives?

"Fuck that. I can get someone a lot better than Piper."

"Why did I ever find you attractive?" Piper groans behind me, resting her head against my back.

"Grow a fucking pair, Duncan. Maybe if you treated women better, you could get a woman like Piper. Thank God she realized she was better than you." I sneer at him.

I want to lay him out for how he treated—still treats—Piper. She doesn't deserve it. But after hearing Coach's earlier words to me, I don't want to do anything to disappoint him.

"It's okay, Cash." Piper squeezes my bicep. "Duncan's opinion doesn't matter."

"Whatever you need to tell yourself to feel better."

"C'mon, Piper." I grab her hand and start to walk down the tunnel. "We don't need to stay here a minute longer."

"Piper." Duncan grabs her by the arm as we walk by.

"Get your fucking hands off her."

Even Duncan touching Piper has me seeing red and ready to lose my mind.

"Cash. Don't."

"You should listen to her."

Duncan is staring me straight in the eye. His green eyes look like burned moss. Probably because the man is void of any emotion.

"Duncan—" I'm seething. If I could punch him and get away with it right now, I would.

"He's not going to treat you right." He ignores me, addressing Piper.

"What, and you did?" she fires back.

That's my spitfire of a Princess. She doesn't need a Prince Charming to rescue her. She can fight her own battles.

Not that I'll ever let her do battle on her own. Not against Duncan. She doesn't have to.

"Better than he ever will."

"Duncan, you don't get a say in this."

"You realize why he'll never settle down, right?"

"Oh yeah? Why's that?" Piper crosses her arms, leveling him with a stare that has him taking a step back.

"Willy has never settled down because he doesn't care about people. I know how many puck bunnies he has in every city we play in."

"He's not the one that cheated on me!" Piper snaps.

Green eyes stare down at her. Piper backs up a step into me. A silent plea for strength.

"Grow up, Piper. He's a hockey player. We're all the same." Duncan wears a smarmy grin on his face.

I wonder if I could pay someone on our next rival team to punch his perfect teeth out.

"No, Duncan, you're not all the same. You use your status to sleep with anyone on two legs. Cash is a good man."

Duncan shoves off the wall, getting ready to leave.

"You're kidding yourself, Piper. Cash is just like every other hockey player. You're delusional if you think you can change him. Whatever you think you have, it's not real. I hope you're prepared to get your heart broken."

With a wink at Piper, he's gone.

"Duncan!" I shout after him as he heads back down the hallway with a whistle.

"Deep breaths, Cash."

Piper's hands hold me back.

"You can't let him talk to you like that," I grit out.

"It doesn't matter."

"It doesn't?" I turn to face her. "Why not?"

Piper clasps my cheeks between her hands and pulls my focus to her. Her blue eyes are fierce.

Deep breaths, Cash. Deep breaths.

"Because I know the truth."

"And what's the truth?" Another deep breath.

"Duncan is a dick."

"I know." I smirk.

"The truth is," Piper starts, thumbs brushing against my jaw, "I know what kind of man you really are. And it's not going to be undone by some lies that Duncan carelessly throws around."

"No?"

She shakes her head. "You are a good man, Cash Williams. You don't have countless women spread across the country. You'd rather go home to your dog every night."

"Well, and you."

Piper smiles, settling the rage that is stewing inside of me. "And me. Ignore him. You're better than that."

The faith Piper has in me is unwavering. Something I've never had before in my life. Everything was always conditional growing up.

Win a game. *You didn't do enough.*

Lose a game. *It was your fault for getting into a fight.*

Get into a fight. *You let them beat you.*

With Piper, I don't have to do anything but be myself.

Without thinking, I sweep her back into my arms and give her a kiss, one that tries to convey everything I'm feeling.

I've never been good at that. But based on her whimpers, I think she can feel it.

We'll be back from the All-Star break in a few weeks. And when we're back in Denver, I'm going to find a way to tell her. My focus needs to be on hockey until then.

After?

I'll tell her I'm falling for her.

No, fallen for her.

I want Piper Fields, and if I have anything to say about it, she'll be mine.

PIPER

PIPER

You looked great at the skills competition!

CASH THE SEX GOD

Thanks, Princess

Cash! When did you change your name in my phone?!

I knew you'd like it

I can't with you

You can't deny it's true

I might...

Then I might hold out on you

Fine. You're Cash the Sex God <<eye roll emoji>>

Oh, Princess, you say the sweetest things to me <<kissing face emoji>>

I try. What's next on the agenda?

I've got a meet and greet with fans tomorrow

I wish I could be there.

You'll be here soon

I miss you

I miss you too. I wish I could go out with you

Angie and I have a few things planned

You'll have fun

Not as much fun without you <<sad face emoji>>

Just you wait…I have all the fun things planned when I see you again

Great, now I need to use the vibrator

Princess, you cannot tell me that

Turnabout is fair play

Fine. Then I need to go take a long cold shower

Think of me <<kissing face emoji>>

You know I do, Princess

"Is this your first time in Nashville?" Angie expertly dodges a group of people on Broadway as we navigate our way to the bar.

"Yeah. I wish we had more time here."

Neon lights fight for attention on both sides of the closed-off street. Music filters out from every bar we pass, mostly hopeful singers wanting a contract to become the next big thing. There's more people crowded on this street than I've ever seen in my life.

"If only Harper were here this week."

"Where's she this week?" I ask, nearly running into someone who stumbles out of a bar. Angie tried to make plans for us to meet up with one of her closest friends, but she wasn't in town this weekend.

"It's her mom's birthday, so she made a long weekend of it at home."

"Can't say I'd want to be here with so many people."

Angie laughs as she finds the bar we're looking for and guides us inside. "She's used to this. Not sure if she's used to this many hockey fans."

"Even if we don't like the Knights, it's not a bad spot to have the All-Star Game."

Angie sidles up to the bar, finding a small break in the people to order us drinks. White wine for her and an old fashioned for me.

"Are you excited about Cash's first All-Star Game?"

"Is it weird I'm nervous?" I ask her, a bit louder than necessary given the number of people in here.

Two drinks are dropped off and Angie pulls out two twenties to pay him.

Angie links her arm through mine as we walk through the crowded bar toward a quiet table in the back, trying not to spill our drinks.

The bar is packed, wall-to-wall with hockey fans with various jerseys from all the teams represented. A country tune plays as people dance to the music.

It's everything a Nashville bar should be.

"I was nervous for Troy's first one, but not anymore."

"Do you get used to it?" I ask.

Not that I should get used to it. Because Cassie said after the All-Star break, we were done. Cash's image has rebounded with the press.

Snarky comments after games? None.

Getting into fights on the ice? Only when they really deserve it.

Sweet and attentive boyfriend? Check and check.

"It's not as bad during the regular season," Angie tells me, sipping on her wine. "But the playoffs? I'm a ball of nerves the entire time."

I laugh. If only Cash and I would make it that far.

"I don't think I could handle that."

"You'll have me by your side. Don't worry."

"Good."

Angie has become a good friend these last few months. We never really hung out before I started working for the team and dating Cash. Now? Now, she's someone I can talk to about anything.

Well, almost anything. Because no one can know that this thing with Cash has an expiration date.

"I still can't believe Duncan got into the game."

Angie snorts over her glass of wine. "I don't know how you dated him."

"Can we say it was a lapse in judgment?"

"Believe me, I've had those."

I clap my hand over hers on the table between us. "And now you're married."

A dreamy look washes over her face. It's the same look she had on her face when she married Troy. One of pure blissed-out love.

"Do you ever think about you and Cash getting married?"

It's an innocent enough question, but it has my heart sinking. "I haven't thought about it."

"Then why do you look so sad right now?"

"I don't know if Cash is the marrying type."

Angie waves me off. "I've seen the way he looks at you. It's in the cards."

"He doesn't look at me like that at all."

"Piper. Please. Of course he does. That is the look of love. He is head over heels for you. Well, head over skates," she says on a laugh.

Love? There is no way it's the look of love.

I can't love Cash. I couldn't possibly be in love with him, could I? I told myself I couldn't fall for him. Cash isn't the boyfriend type. We're only doing this so he can bounce back in the eyes of the press so it helps him with the team.

Cash doesn't do love. He's told me as much. I don't want to get my hopes up.

The music of the bar presses in around me, bringing me back to reality.

"Even if we do, it's a long way off."

"I told Troy that. That I wanted to wait to get married."

"And you got married, what, after his second season?"

She nods, tucking a stray strand of dark hair behind her ear. "I didn't know why I was waiting. It was ridiculous."

"I'm only twenty-two. I'm in no rush."

Even if I did want to marry Cash, and I'm not saying I do, it feels too young to get married. I'm not even done getting my master's degree yet. There's still so much I want to do.

"I won't keep bugging you about it," Angie tells me. "We have an All-Star Game tonight!"

"That we do!"

I swallow down the rest of my old fashioned and put more excitement into my voice than I feel. Because Angie has all sorts of thoughts swirling around in my head.

Love.

Marriage.

Cash.

All the things that the two of us won't get. Because Cash Williams is a lone wolf. Someone who doesn't need anyone.

If only Cash could need me.

"We should get going if we're going to beat the crowds."

"Let's go."

I slip into my jacket, letting it hang open over Cash's jersey. Because even if we're going to be done soon, I am still proud to be his.

Even for a little while.

Chapter Twenty-Three

"**I** know this game doesn't mean anything in the standings, but I want them to win so badly," I tell Angie. We're in a suite with a few other players' wives, but no one I know.

"Because you want them to be the better team and win. Best of the best."

"I still can't believe Cash got in. I mean, I can, but I can't."

"Believe it, Piper. He's going to help the team make a run for the playoffs when the season picks back up."

"You're really going to have to help me deal with those nerves when it happens."

Angie stands, giving me a warm smile. "You know I'm here for you. I'm going to grab a drink. Need anything?"

I shake my head. "Just a water."

"You got it."

The intermission is going by with the teams' mascots playing a round of musical chairs on the ice. I take the time to settle my brain with mindless scrolling, looking through past text messages with Cash.

All the way back to when this thing started. It's hard to believe how much time has passed, yet it's still flown by.

Pictures of the two of us.

Puck.

Articles talking about how he's an asset to Colorado.

Sexy texts.

Those are my favorite and ones I should not be looking at in public.

But with the All-Star break ending with the game tonight, we don't really have a reason to keep this thing going. Cassie said this weekend was it. It's hard not to look at everything we had and hope for more.

Because…do we really have to give this thing up?

I know Cash is a loner, doesn't like people. I'm hoping that maybe he's changed his mind. That when we get home we can have a conversation about making this thing permanent.

I'm not ready to let go of Cash.

"Enjoying the game?"

My phone flies out of my hand as Ava chirps in my ear. She pops a piece of popcorn into her mouth with a smile on her face that has ice sliding through me.

"I thought you weren't coming?"

How Duncan got into the game, I still don't know.

"Duncan changed his mind. I'm glad he did. Who knew seeing you here would be so fun?"

"Sure you don't want something stronger?" Angie asks, eyes glaring at Ava as she retakes her seat.

"I'm good."

"Nothing for me," Ava tells her, like she was offering to get her something.

"Excuse me, are you Angie Hollins?" A woman comes up to Angie from the bar.

"I am."

"Hi. My husband plays for Nashville and does work with Team Rainbow, and I just wanted to introduce myself."

"Of course!"

Angie pops up from her seat to go talk with her. Ava is rolling her eyes at them. "God, some people are just so… what's the right word? *Fake.*"

Dread settles in my stomach. "What are you talking about?"

Ava rests her elbow on the armrest between us, and her chin on a closed fist. Her brown eyes are menacing as they roll over me.

"Don't play dumb, sweetheart. It's really not a good look. You know what I'm talking about."

"What?"

"You know, you shouldn't read things in public for anyone to see. Tsk tsk."

Oh God. The teams come back onto the ice for the start of the second period. Instead of being excited for the action to start again, I'm ready to crawl into a hole and die.

Ava saw what I was looking at?

"Piper, you okay?" Angie's back and has a worried look on her face. The two of us sitting together would be worrisome for anyone who knows my history with Ava.

"I'm good." I swallow around the lie that slips out. "Ava and I need to go chat for a minute."

I squeeze by Angie and slip out of the suite, finding a quiet corner to have this conversation.

"What in the hell are you doing, Ava?" I hiss at her as she saunters toward me.

She twirls a strand of black hair around her finger. A bedazzled jersey stretches tight across her chest, clashing with the leather pants she's wearing.

"You know," she starts, looking me up and down with a scathing look, "I don't understand how you keep getting these guys to fall for you. But then I realized, it's all fake. Clearly you're lying to get everyone to love Cash, and Duncan? Well, I don't know what he ever saw in you."

"What do you want, Ava?"

"Break up with him."

"What?" I rear back as if she slapped me. "With Cash?"

Ava rolls her eyes at me. "God, you're such a blonde. Yes, with Cash."

"But why?"

Ava takes a step forward, and I retreat farther back into the corner. I can't stand breathing in the smell of her perfume.

"You have been a thorn in my side since I started dating Duncan."

"You mean when you were cheating with him?"

She waves my words off. "Something about you keeps pulling Duncan back. And now I know why."

"Why's that?" I cross my arms, trying to keep my insides where they should be. My stomach has plummeted to my feet, and my heart is threatening to beat out of my chest.

"He wants what he can't have. And based on how your relationship started with Cash, I see an opportunity."

"Can't you let us be?" I plead. "We have nothing to do with your relationship."

"If you're not dating Cash, then Duncan will want nothing to do with you and will want me."

"God, Ava! Are you even hearing yourself? Why would you want to be with someone who doesn't want to be with you?"

"Duncan doesn't know what he wants."

"So how do you know he wants you?"

Ava taps a bright blue nail against my forehead. "Because when he sees me in his room tonight, he'll change his mind."

"Ugh."

That's the last thing I want to be thinking about right now.

"And by the time we get home, you'll have dumped Cash and all will be right in the world."

"What if I don't?"

"Don't break up with Cash?"

I nod.

Ava leans in close. I can smell the gum on her breath. "Then I'll tell everyone that what you two had was fake to win over the media."

Bile rises in my throat. It would serve her right for me to puke all over her designer shoes.

"Why are you doing this?"

"To get what I want."

"I don't want Duncan, Ava!" I shout. A few people are lingering near the restrooms and turn to face us. The last thing I need is for people to find out about me and Cash from my big mouth.

"But I do!" she hisses. "And until you're no longer the forbidden fruit he can't have, I won't be able to have his entire heart."

"So I break up with Cash and that's it? You keep my secret?"

A wicked smile takes over her face. It's ugly. Cunning. Cutting so deep that I feel it down to my bones.

"Yes. If you want your pretty little boy toy to stay with the Black Diamonds, you'll do as I say."

"Ava—"

Ava walks backward, wiggling her fingers at me. "I

know you'll make the right decision, Piper. Break up with him or the world finds out the truth."

I have no claim on Duncan. I never felt a fraction for him of what I feel for Cash. I didn't know I could have feelings this big until Cash came along.

And now?

Now I have to break both our hearts in order to protect him.

Cash has done a one-eighty in the press. They are eating out of the palm of his hand. Anytime the two of us show up on social media, they're talking about what a well-balanced player he is. How his presence has helped the entire team and how it'll carry them through a playoff run.

I don't see any other way out of this.

Tears well in my eyes as I sink into the corner.

I can't even focus on the game now.

I can delete our text conversation, but with one anony-mous source, it'll be spewed all over the tabloids and Cassie would have a nightmare of a time trying to clean it up.

How could I have been so careless to be flipping through our messages where anyone could see?

There's still one period left to play. I have no idea how I'm going to pull myself together to make it through tonight.

Better yet, I don't know how I'm going to make a deci-sion on what to do.

We were going to break up regardless, so why not end it and make a clean break of it?

What a conniving bitch she is. It's not enough that she's ruined my life once already, but now she has to ruin it again.

God, what am I going to do?

Sucking in a deep breath, I try to push every thought

out of my head to make it through the rest of the game. Rainbows and unicorns and princesses.

Princess.

I hear it in Cash's low rumble and it makes my heart crack. I don't know if I'm going to be able to manage this.

I peek my head inside the suite, making sure Ava isn't in there before grabbing another drink at the bar.

"Make it a double, please."

The bartender doesn't think twice as she passes over my drink. I take a healthy swallow before heading back to the suite.

"Piper, are you okay?" Angie asks, as I drop into the seat next to her. The score is tied, with the second period almost over.

"I…"

I don't know how to answer. I'm so far from okay, I'm not even in the same realm. It's the truth.

My heart is slowly breaking as I stare out at the ice. Cash is out there, skating with ease, not a care in the world.

I don't know what's going to happen with Cash and me, but a decision needs to be made.

If I have to break up with him to protect him, I will.

Fucking Duncan. I never should have dated him to start with.

He's done nothing but ruin my life since the moment I met him.

"Piper, you're worrying me."

I wave Angie off. What could I tell her? This thing with Cash started out as a PR scheme to win over the press and now I fell in love with him, but my ex-roommate is threatening to tell everyone that it was fake to make my ex stay with her?

"Must have been something I ate. I'll be fine."

If only…

My insides are a jumbled mess. All I've been thinking about since the All-Star Game is Ava and her words.

Break up with him or the world finds out the truth.

After everything that Cash has done to rehab his image, the very last thing I want is for the world to find out that this was all fake. There is so much goodness inside of him. I want them to know the real Cash.

The one that he is with me. The one he doesn't hide from the world.

"Piper, are you okay?" Claire asks me.

"What?" I jump, turning around to face her. "Why?"

She points to the stack behind me. "You've been folding those towels for every bit of thirty minutes now."

"Oh, sorry."

Folding is generous. They are all piled up in a one big heap. No crisp lines to be seen.

"Do you need a break?" Claire casts a wary eye on me.

"Would you mind? I'm sorry. I didn't sleep well."

"Sure. Twenty minutes and then I want to go over some plans for the next few weeks with you."

"Sounds good." I nod at her before escaping the training room.

It's mercifully empty this time of day. The entire team is out on the ice, letting me escape to the biting, Denver air. I lean against the brick wall, letting it hold me up.

The cold stings my eyes, tears welling almost immediately.

How could I have gotten myself into this situation? Nothing about this plan with Cash was supposed to be permanent. A few months for him to restore his reputation and then we'd quietly go our separate ways.

I didn't plan to fall for him.

I didn't plan on letting him see all my vulnerabilities.

And I definitely didn't plan on giving him my heart.

I thought it hurt when I ended things with Duncan. I don't know if my heart will ever recover from what I know I have to do.

A stray tear slips free and I brush it away with more force than necessary. I don't know how I can possibly break up with Cash. To let him slip free from my life.

The team is gearing up for a playoff push now that the All-Star break is behind them. How can I possibly do this to Cash now? But the warning text from Ava this morning made it crystal clear.

Break things off with him by Friday or she plans on telling the world everything.

How could I have ever been friends with someone so vile?

"Piper?" I jump at the sound of the voice I've fallen in love with.

"Cash? What are you doing out here?"

In two strides, he closes the distance between us. Being

this close to him, smelling him, makes my nose tingle with emotion.

"I had an issue with my skate that the equipment guys needed to look at. What are *you* doing out here?"

He's still in his pads, practice jersey stretching across his chest.

"I…"

This is going to be so much harder than I thought.

"What's going on? Are you okay?"

His warm hand cups my cheek, and I can't take it.

I can't take this man and his tender touch when I'm about ready to kick him to the curb.

"Look, Cash." I suck in a deep breath and force out the words I don't want to say. "This thing is over."

He looks stunned. Like I slapped him across the face.

"What in world are you talking about, Princess?"

"I'm not your Princess anymore," I snap.

The words taste like bile on my lips.

"Piper." Cash's brows draw tight as he looks down at me. "What in the world is going on?"

"Cassie said this thing could end after the All-Star Game." I look around like it's the most obvious thing in the world. "Well, All-Star Game was last week."

"So that's it? This is over?"

I nod, crossing my arms over my chest. Hoping like hell it'll keep my heart in my chest and not let it bleed all over the sidewalk.

"You can't even say the words, can you?"

The look in Cash's eyes could tear down a weaker man. But they can't tear down someone protecting the person they love.

I put as much force behind my words as I can to get them to land.

"We're done."

Cash sucks in a breath and takes a step back from me. "That's it? No discussion about continuing this thing?"

"What's there to continue?"

"What's there to continue?" he parrots back at me. "I don't know; I thought this thing was built on a lot more than Cassie needing to fix my reputation."

I shrug a shoulder, trying to play off his words. "And that's exactly what we did, Cash. What's left to do? You've told me you don't need anyone, so why do you need me?"

Cash scrubs an angry hand across his jaw, turning his back to me. I take my fill of him. Because it will be the last time I ever get him like this.

Cash Williams is the most striking man I've ever met. Sharp jawline. Deep, brown eyes. Shoulders that carry too much weight for any one person.

A heart that's so big, he doesn't know what to do with it except keep it locked up away from the world.

I only got to see it for a short time, but I know the man he is. I only hope that he won't be bitter because of all this.

"You know," Cash starts, dropping his hands to his hips as he paces in front of me, "I thought we had something here. Something more than just Cassie hooking me up with you. For the first time in my life, I let someone in. I let *you* in, Piper. Told you things I've never told anyone."

I bite down on my lip to stop it from quivering. If Cash gets a whiff of how I'm feeling, he'll try to come up with a better plan. But how can he stop Ava from going to the press? She's a narcissist and gets what she wants.

God, I hate her.

"I guess I'm a really good actress."

Cash draws to a stop in front of me. "Well, congratulations. I guess you get the award for being the best fake girlfriend out there and making me fall in love with you."

He storms off in a haze of anger and sadness, not

turning around as he pulls open the door to the arena. Cash doesn't spare a backward glance as he heads inside.

Maybe if he did, I'd collapse into his arms and try to make this right.

The clatter of the door slamming breaks my hold. Every emotion I've been holding inside escapes in a rush. Heaving sobs escape me as I try to get everything under control. It's still early in the day. I have a full day ahead of me that I need to push through.

Except, I didn't plan on breaking Cash's heart today. Or destroying my own.

I pull my phone from the pocket of my team-issued uniform pants. I got this internship because of Noah. And now, the last thing I want is to be working for the Black Diamonds.

The thought of seeing Cash every day and not being able to touch him or kiss him is a hell of my own making.

I shoot a quick text to Ava.

PIPER

It's done.

AVA

Then your secret is safe with me

I STUFF my phone back in my pocket. Taking one last deep breath, I steel my spine. It's going to take everything I have to make it through the day.

Because Cash Williams is no longer mine.

And that is the saddest thing in the world.

Chapter Twenty-Five

"**W**hy aren't you at the game, sweetheart?" Mom asks, handing me a glass of water from over the couch.

"I didn't feel like going tonight."

I'm curled up into a tiny ball, a soft gray blanket pulled over me. It's the first home game after the break, and I couldn't muster the energy to go to the game.

I wouldn't be in the WAGs suite, so why bother?

Dad went to the game with all his friends since Nashville is in town. Graham is Knox's son, so they all have a vested interest in the game. Leaving Mom and me together at home.

"What's the real reason you aren't there?" Mom drops down onto the couch next to me.

My eyes track Cash as he skates down the ice. There's a violence to his game tonight. Like he's out for blood.

Colorado and Nashville have no love lost between the two of them. As evidenced by the hit Noah lays on Graham.

"I'm fine." I sip on my drink, not daring to look at my mom.

"I didn't ask if you were fine, Piper."

The ice cube clinks in my drink as I swirl the water around, hoping it will swallow me down.

"I broke up with Cash."

The gasp from her is audible, causing me to turn and look at her. "What happened?"

My lip quivers, tears gathering in my eyes.

If I never cried again, it would be too soon. Every day after work, I go home and slip into bed with nothing but tears to keep me company.

I spend all my energy keeping it together during the day, so I have nothing left for the rest of the night.

"It wasn't real."

Mom sets her wine glass down, pausing the game in front of us with the camera zoomed in on Cash. He looks so angry, he could spit fire.

"Piper. What are you talking about, it wasn't real?"

"It was all a PR stunt to fix his reputation."

I gulp down the rest of my drink and head back to the kitchen. If I'm going to have this conversation right now, I need liquid courage.

Mom stalks after me, not letting me pour the bourbon into my empty glass.

"I saw the two of you together," she tells me. "How could what the two of you had *not* be real?"

"Because it wasn't!" I snap.

I bury my fists into my eyes. Every single thought has been consumed by Cash Williams. His scent that still lingers in my apartment. The Post-It note he wrote me that is still stuck to my fridge. Hell, I can't even get away from him while watching my team play.

"Piper, look at me."

"No." Because if I do, I'll burst into tears. Not that I'm doing that good of a job of keeping it together.

"Honey." Mom pulls my hands down and forces me to look at her. I am her mirror image. From the blonde hair and the blue eyes right down to the smile and dimple on the left cheek. "Tell me what happened. Because if you broke up with him for the reason you said you did, you wouldn't be this upset."

The tenderness in her words has the dam breaking. "I...I..."

"Oh, sweetheart."

She pulls me in for a hug and holds me as I cry. Buckets of tears fall as I try to suck in deep breaths to no avail. Mom strokes my hair, holding me close.

The only thing that calms me down is the faint scent of strawberries from the lotion that Mom always uses.

"Deep breaths. Deep breaths," she whispers into my ear.

I nod, sucking them in the best I can. Mom guides me back to the couch and pulls me down into her arms.

"Can you tell me what happened?"

And I do. I spill everything to her.

"In the span of a few months, I went from having a boyfriend, to him cheating on me with my roommate and dumping me, to actually finding a boyfriend that I love when it wasn't supposed to be real and then being threatened by the ex's current girlfriend that she'll ruin everything if I don't break up with Cash so Duncan doesn't want me anymore."

It comes out in a rush, but it's the only way I can get it out.

"That's a lot to unpack there."

"How do I keep getting myself into these situations?" I mutter into my mom's arms.

"I have a question," Mom tells me.

"Only one?" I laugh, wiping away the tears. My eyes burn from all the crying.

She smirks at me, tucking a stray piece of hair behind my ear. "Fine. The first question. How do you really feel about Cash?"

My eyes flit to the TV where it's still paused on his face. He's like the sun, pulling me in. Not letting me go. "I love him."

It's the easiest words I've ever said.

"Then why didn't you talk to him to try and figure this out?"

"I had to make it believable." With Ava flitting about the arena, she would've caught on if we were pretending. And that would've screwed everything else up.

"Oh, sweetheart. Maybe try talking to Cassie. See if there's anything she can do?"

Her tone is hopeful, but I don't know what she would be able to do.

"Maybe."

"So you're just going to be brokenhearted for the rest of your life? If I did that, I wouldn't have you."

"Ugh, Mom. I don't want to hear about your and Dad's love life."

Mom couldn't stop her smile if she tried. "All I'm saying is if I didn't forgive your father all those years ago, we wouldn't be here."

"Can we talk about something else?"

The thought of love right now makes me sick.

"Fine." Mom flips the game off and turns on an old rerun of *Friends*.

"You don't want to watch the game?"

"There's no sense in making you more miserable tonight by watching the game."

"You know you're the best mom, right?"

I don't know the last time she's missed one of Noah's games. When we were growing up, she was always there. Even now, she's at almost every home game they have. She's a hockey mom through and through, rarely missing a game.

She drops a kiss on my head and pulls me into her arms again. A place I will gladly stay to feel safe for the night. Comforted. Like my whole world isn't crashing down on me.

"And don't you ever forget it."

Chapter Twenty-Six

CASH

"You ready, Willy? Feeling good?" the trainer asks as he wraps my ribs.

"Feeling fine."

I don't need him to keep checking in on me. My ribs feel fine. My entire body feels fine on the ice.

It's about the only damn thing that does.

Because for the last two weeks, I've been nothing but a sad sack.

Piper dumping me was a crushing blow I didn't see coming. Maybe I should have because she avoided me when we got back from Nashville. I thought we could talk about the two of us continuing our relationship for real.

I guess it never meant anything to her.

I shake the thoughts of her away and finish getting ready for the game.

"You going to be okay tonight?" Strawberry asks.

"How many times are you guys going to ask me that?"

"You've been in a funk ever since—"

"Don't say it," I snap. "I know what happened. I was there."

"Look, don't bite my head off, but we need your head in the game tonight, okay?"

"I'll be fine," I bite out.

I don't even look at him. Because when I see him, I'll see Piper. And then I'll get angry all over again.

Thankfully, years of practice have burned the pregame warm-ups into my brain like they're second nature. I shoot pucks at the goal, watching half slide on by the pipes.

God. Tonight is going to be harder than I first thought.

I stand on the ice, watching the flag as the national anthems ring out, and try to quell my thoughts.

Hockey.

It's the one thing that will never let me down.

Well, that and Puck. Except every time he looks at me now, I sense his judgment. Like I did something to scare off the woman we both love.

The puck drops and I lock down my emotions. Troy gains easy control of the puck but Vancouver is there. Noah tries to block the defenseman, but they're able to steal the puck and move it down the ice toward our zone.

Fuck.

Our defense sets up, trying to stop the play from unfolding but it doesn't work. Vancouver catches us off guard and sinks one in the net.

The home crowd goes wild.

"Look alive out there, Willy," Duncan chirps.

"Fuck you!" I shout back.

I don't have it in me to control my temper tonight. Not when I'm so low right now.

The first period is more of the same. And the second.

By the time the third period rolls around, we're down 3-1.

Duncan swipes the puck from Vancouver and a defenseman is on him within seconds.

"Pass the puck!"

My pleas go unheard. Duncan ignores the fact that I'm open and fires the puck at Vancouver's goal. It bounces off the goalie's shin pads, and a winger for the Lightning scoops up the puck and returns to our end of the ice.

He's on a breakaway. No matter how hard I push myself, I can't catch up to him. The puck flies toward the net and sails past Nick.

Fuck.

The crowd explodes around us as the horn blasts through the arena.

Vancouver is up 4-1 late in the third. With the way we've been playing tonight, there's no way we're going to make up the deficit.

Duncan skates past me to hit the bench. "Where are you, Williams? You're sluggish tonight."

"Me? You're the one who didn't pass the puck to me earlier!"

"Because you've been playing like shit." He gets up in my face.

"And maybe if you were more of a team player, I would've been able to score."

I'm seething with anger. I don't think I've ever been this pissed off during a game. What the fuck is wrong with this guy?

"Guys. Cameras are watching." Troy skates between the two of us as he heads out to center ice to take the ensuing faceoff.

I take my spot on the bench. Far away from fuckface Duncan. I can't believe I'm on the same line as him. He's a mediocre player at best and proved it by hogging the puck and losing an easy scoring opportunity.

I take a swig from my water bottle, trying to cool down. There's no point in getting worked up. Nothing is going to happen. Duncan is going to keep being a tool and selfish with the puck.

Coach Barney is walking down the bench, trying to pump up the team. "We've still got time, boys. Williams," — he looks at me—"Hanson is weak on the left side, so if you see your chance, take it."

"You got it, Coach."

Not like I haven't been trying to beat them there all night. Vancouver is putting up one hell of a fight tonight.

Troy and Noah are doing everything they can, but to no avail. We end up losing 5-2. One pitiful goal to close out the third period.

I make it through postgame interviews without losing my cool. Cleaning up, I change back into my suit and head toward the team bus.

"We're going to hit the bars." Troy walks up next to me on the long walk outside. I pull my coat tighter around me. The wind is biting in Vancouver tonight.

"I really don't want to," I groan. It was a hard-fought game. And to come out with a loss makes it even harder.

"The little lady got you on a short leash?" Duncan slams into my shoulder as he walks past me.

"Fuck off, man."

After my night, I want to head back to the hotel and call Piper.

But I can't.

Because we're not together anymore.

"You don't have to if you don't want to," Troy tells me as we walk out of the arena. Vancouver fans are lingering, and a few boos escape from them.

"Don't you want to call Angie?" I ask, dropping my bag onto the sidewalk to get loaded onto the bus.

"Nah. We talked earlier. She's going out with some friends from work tonight."

"Fine."

"Good." Troy looks smug. "If you'd have said no, I would've dragged your ass out anyway."

I collapse onto the seat and wait for the rest of the guys to get on.

It's like I'm moving through quicksand. Everything is moving around me but I barely notice it.

Is this what heartbreak feels like? Because I did not sign up for this.

Before I can change my mind and head to my hotel room once we arrive, Troy steers me toward a small bar across the street.

"I hate you."

"Noted and ignored."

He waves down the bartender and orders a round before heading to a private area. Knowing him, he called ahead for us to have a quiet area to wallow.

"Alright, drink up, Willy. You're making me sad," Troy tells me, handing me a shot and a beer.

"I am sad." Knocking back the shot, the tequila burns.

One shot won't kill me. Maybe it'll dull the pain enough to make this next stretch of road games bearable.

"Are you going to be like this the rest of the season?" Nick asks, leaning back in his chair with a glass of water. I don't think I've ever seen the kid drink.

"What's it to you?"

Nick rolls his eyes, tipping forward. "If you're this upset, talk to her."

"I've tried calling her. She keeps ignoring me."

"What'd you do?" Noah asks. "I saw you two at Christmas. It was disgusting."

"Gee, thanks."

"I'm serious. What happened?"

I grab another shot from the table and swallow it down

followed by a sip of beer. "I don't know. I was ready to take things to the next level with her after the All-Star Game and then the next thing I know, she's dumping me."

"Did you not pay enough attention to her?" Noah asks.

"That can't be it," Nick says.

"I agree." This being Troy. "Angie told me how cute they are together."

"I don't think I asked for a breakdown on where my relationship went wrong with you losers tonight," I interject.

"Aww," Troy says, "he really does love us."

I flip him the bird.

"I need some ass tonight," Duncan's voice carries over our small group. He's hanging out with Rio behind us. No one else wants to go near him tonight after his shitty play.

"Ignore him," Noah tells me.

"You really sent Ava packing?"

That perks me up.

"She thought I was still hung up on my ex. Tried to blackmail both of us so that I'd stay with her. I don't need a chick that badly."

"Did you hear that?" I ask Noah.

"What in the fuck is he talking about?" he whispers.

"Blackmail? Are you in a Bond movie?" Rio laughs.

"Nah. I told her that I don't need that amount of crazy in my life. Besides, I have a new chick."

"Of course you do. I bow down to the master."

I can't listen to this anymore. Turning around, I face Duncan, who is already buzzed.

"What in the fuck are you talking about?" I ask him.

"What's it to you?" He crosses his arms, one ankle resting against the other knee.

Grabbing him by his shirt, I haul him up to me. "What in the fuck did you do to Piper?"

After hearing his words, I know he had something to do with it. For the first time since I've known him, Duncan doesn't look cocky, but scared.

I can't imagine the look on my face. It's what happens when you fucking mess with me and the woman I love.

Because even though she dumped me, I still love Piper. More than I'll ever love anyone else.

"Ava knew the truth about you two."

Oh fuck.

"And?" I shake him.

"Thought that if Piper dumped you, I wouldn't want her anymore and only want Ava. Not that I did. Want Piper." His words are slurring together. "Which I told her after she threatened Piper at the All-Star Game."

"Un-fucking-believable."

"Look man, I sent her packing. That's too much crazy for me."

"Fuck off, Douche." I push him away from me. "You're fucking up everyone's lives with your shit."

"I've had enough of your shit."

Duncan tries to throw a punch at me, but it glances off my jaw before Noah and Troy are jumping in.

"What the fuck, Duncan?"

As many times as I've wanted to punch this guy, I just don't have it in me now. Because I know how disappointed Piper would be in me.

"Take him back to the hotel!" Troy shouts at Rio. "We can't have this shit here."

Thank God for the private room, otherwise who knows how many cameras would be aimed our way?

I sink down into a cushioned booth, holding my jaw. It's tender, but thankfully not much else.

My heart is still the most battered thing inside me.

"You dumbass." Noah stands over me, handing me a

bag of ice. "You just couldn't punch him? Just once for all of us?"

I huff out a laugh, pressing the ice against my jaw. "I couldn't bring myself to do it."

"So all that shit he said…is it true?"

I shrug a shoulder. "It has to be, right? If Ava threatened Piper, it's the only thing I can think that would make Piper dump me."

"And why would she dump you to protect you?"

"Cassie concocted this whole plan to help my image with the press by having me date Piper."

"It was fake?" Noah asks.

I nod. Swiping my beer from the table, I take a hearty sip.

"I don't buy it."

"It's true."

Noah punches me in the shoulder.

"Dude. I've already taken enough hits tonight."

"Sorry." He holds up his hands. "But I saw the two of you together. My sister loves you. And you love her, if you wearing that ugly sweater has anything to say about it."

I swirl the beer in my glass, watching the foam on top fizzle out. "I do. I love her. I didn't want it to happen, but I do."

"Then fucking fight for her, man. She's dated nothing but losers and douches-"

"Literally," I laugh, interrupting him.

"Are you going to let Duncan win? Because I for one don't want to put up with your mopey ass for the rest of the season. And hers."

"You've seen her?" I perk up at that.

"I talked to her on the phone for five minutes and she told me she was fine about twenty times."

"Sounds like her."

"Then what are you going to do, Cash? Fight for her, or give up and let Duncan win?"

Chapter Twenty-Seven

PIPER

Today was easy. Well, easier. With the team being on the road, it made it easier to breathe. But I know they got back this afternoon. I was able to sneak away early and get home before the emotions started to take over under the ruse of working on my final project.

Shouldering my way into my apartment, I'm met with a sight I never expected.

Cash standing in my living room.

"What in the world are you doing here?"

Under his eyes, it looks like he has purple thumbprints. The team was only on a three-game road trip on the west coast before coming back. He shouldn't look this tired.

I hate that he is this way.

Cash flashes the spare key my brother has in case of emergency. "You and I need to have a conversation."

"Cash, I don't think we do." I shut my door and drop my purse onto the entry table. So much for trying to keep everything in check tonight.

"Sorry, Princess, you don't get a say in this."

"I don't?" I turn to face him. He's moved into the kitchen.

He's still in his away-game attire, sans tie. The tattoos on his chest peek out from where his shirt is unbuttoned.

Cash shakes his head, holding a hand out to me. "See, I couldn't figure out why you would break things off between us."

I take his hand and he pulls me into him. He's a solid wall of mass that I've missed way too much in the last two weeks.

"I did—"

"I know why you did it." Cash drops a finger over my lips.

"You do?" I mumble against his finger.

He nods. "Ava."

I suck in a breath. "But how?"

Cash backs us up into the living room, sitting me on the couch. He drops between my knees, pulling me to the edge in his arms.

"Duncan."

"What?" Now I'm really confused.

"He was being a douche and bragging about dumping Ava because she was too crazy and blackmailing him. He kept bragging about it to Rio and I was able to put the pieces together."

I pick at a loose thread on my pants. Embarrassment creeps up my cheeks.

Cash tips my chin up, forcing me to look him dead in the eyes. "Why didn't you come to me when Ava found out?"

"Because what could anyone do? I couldn't let Ava destroy your reputation!" I explode, bursting up from the couch in a fit of rage. "It was my fault! I was reading our texts and she saw them and put two and two together.

You've worked so hard to let people see the real you, and any hint of a scandal would blow that wide open. I couldn't let her do that to you!"

Cash is smiling. A full-blown, irritatingly handsome smile that I love. Damn him for being so sexy when I'm angry.

"So what?"

That stops me in my tracks. "I had to protect you!"

Cash stands, approaching me like a wounded animal. "Piper. I'm a grown-ass man and capable of taking care of myself."

"You shouldn't have to. I want to be able to take care of you. And I never want anyone to see you for less than you are."

"Is that how you see me, Piper?"

I bite my lip, trying to keep my emotions in check. "Yes."

Cash lifts me into his arms and pushes me against the wall. "I don't need you to protect me. I should be the one protecting you from those two idiots."

Cash's nose brushes against mine. Too many emotions are flitting through his eyes. "I want everyone to see you like I do. The kind, caring, loving man you are. I never want people to think badly of you because you were only dating me to make them see that."

He shakes his head. "You think I was only dating you for that reason?"

"Yes?" There's uncertainty in my voice.

"Do I need to teach you a lesson, Princess? I never do anything I don't want to do. And being with you is the one thing in the world I want more than anything."

"But how?" My heart is battering against my ribs. "Ava will—"

"Ava is no longer in the picture."

"What happened?"

The smile Cash gives me is one that I will savor for the rest of my life. "Duncan sent her packing."

"But she could still spill our secret."

"We'll talk to Cassie. It'll be okay."

"She hates me though. What if she tells the media?"

Cash shakes his head. "Then let her. I'm not going to let her stop me from being with the woman I love."

"Even after everything I did?"

"Even after everything you did. We're in this together, Princess. If someone comes at me, we deal with it together. I only wish I had gotten a hit in on Duncan."

"Did he do this?" I brush my fingers against the faint mark on his jaw.

"You'd be so proud of me, not going after him like he deserved."

"You still could," I tell him.

"I'd rather spend my time with you. If you'll still have me."

I cup Cash's cheeks in my hands. Stubble lines his cheeks, heavier than normal. That emotion in his eyes? It's easy to pinpoint. It's love. Love for me. Even after everything I put the two of us through.

"Cash Williams, I'll have you any way I can. I love you more than I ever thought possible."

"Yeah?" he asks, smile playing on his lips.

"Yes."

"Good. Then let me show you how much I love you."

Cash takes my lips in the sweetest kiss of my life. His tongue glides along the seam of my lips and I open for him. I downright whimper at how good his tongue feels against mine.

I thought I lost this. Lost him. I don't know how I could

have ever given him up. Two weeks in hell of my own personal making.

Each pass of his tongue on mine is like the two of us relearning each other. Of wiping out the memories of everyone else.

Only us. Forever.

All too soon, he's pulling away.

"Cash..." I groan.

"Easy, Princess. I have something for you."

Cash walks us backward toward the bed and places me gently on top of the soft duvet. "What could you possibly get me that I don't already have?"

He presses another quick kiss to me, but I grab onto his shirt and hold him there.

"I realized that no one has ever shown up for you. So this is me showing up for you."

"What?"

Cash pulls out a bag that I didn't notice before. Sitting next to it is a vase of my favorite flowers with a tin of cookies from my favorite bakery.

"No one has ever put you first. They've treated you less than the Princess you are, and I realize I haven't been showing you just how much you mean to me."

A bottle of my favorite bourbon is in the bag. A picture of the two of us with Puck at Christmas in what looks to be a homemade frame with 'Cash <3s Piper' scrawled across the top.

It's all of my favorite things.

Everything I love including the man for me.

"Cash." Emotion laces my voice. For the first time in two weeks, it's not tinged with sadness, but happiness. A happiness so bright, it's blooming and threatening to burst out.

"I love you, Princess. Every day I will show you just how much I do. You deserve it."

"Oh, Cash. I don't need this. All I need is you."

I pull him toward me in a bruising kiss. A kiss that seals the love the two of us have together. A promise for the future.

Cash and I make quick work of our clothes before he's sinking in to me. Before long, he's exploding inside of me. Making me come on a quiet gasp that has my entire body yearning to be as close as possible to him.

A tear slides out of my eye.

"Princess." He drops his forehead to mine.

"I love you, Cash. I love you so much, it's hard to breathe."

Cash kisses my tears away. "I'll never get tired of hearing you say that, Piper. I love you."

Cash pulls the duvet over us, and it's a moment I'll commit to my memory for the rest of time.

Nothing about this relationship is fake. It's as real as they come.

Because Cash Williams is my knight in shining armor. My Prince Charming.

The love of my life.

And I can't wait to spend every minute with him.

Chapter Twenty-Eight

CASH

"You know, Piper, you really could have come to me with this." Cassie turns an eye on Piper.

"I didn't want them to do anything to Cash." She shies away from the confrontation.

Cassie clasps her hands over her desk and leans toward Piper. "And who do you think has the power to make them keep their mouths shut?"

"Uhh…" Piper stammers.

"That's right, me." Her eyes flit to mine. "You both should have come to me."

I throw my hands up in defense. "Hey, I didn't know about this until last night. I came to you immediately."

"Way to throw me under the bus," Piper mutters.

"Hey." I grab her hand. "I want them to go away as much as you do, Princess. Okay?"

I kiss her palm, and Cassie's eyes are bugging out of her head when I look at her again.

"You know you don't have to pretend when you're with me, right?"

I smile at Piper. "We know. But this isn't fake. Not anymore."

"Wow." Cassie throws a pen down on her desk and leans back in her chair. "Who knew my brilliant idea would work."

"This was your plan the whole time?" Piper asks.

"I mean, I didn't think it would last, but Cash is a changed man."

I roll my eyes at her. "Thanks, Cassie."

"I'm serious. I wouldn't have picked Piper if I didn't think you two would be good together. Maybe I should start a matchmaking business…" Cassie trails off.

"Back to the matter at hand…"

Piper wants to get down to business.

Cassie stacks the papers strewn about on her desk. "Well, we won't have to do much in the way of Duncan."

"Why not? Ava will still be a problem." Piper squeezes my hand. I know she's nervous. It's why she broke up with me in the first place.

To protect me.

As much as I hated that she did it, I understand why.

I love her all the more for it.

"Duncan has been cut from the Black Diamonds."

"What?" Piper and I ask in unison.

Cassie glances between the two of us. "You really didn't see the news?"

"No. Tell us."

"Conduct detrimental to the team."

"What does that mean?" Piper asks.

Cassie's smile is way too big for what she's telling us.

"He was caught screwing the assistant coach's wife."

My jaw drops. "No fucking way."

"I believe it." Piper sits back in her chair and crosses her arms. "Duncan will screw anything with two legs."

"Is it bad I'm glad he's gone?" I ask.

"I'll be cleaning up that mess for a while," Cassie tells us. "For once, you will not be the biggest pain in my ass, Cash."

"Glad to give you a reprieve." I laugh.

"Maybe you could keep it up. Stay out of my hair for a while?"

I glance over at the woman sitting to my right. The woman that has stolen my heart. Her smile has my chest full to the point it could burst.

"I think I can plan on that."

"Good. Now get out of my office. I have to release a statement on why our assistant coach and winger were let go."

"Wait," Piper interjects, "Coach Cooper was let go too?"

Cassie nods. "Yes. We couldn't let him keep his position after what happened and his behavior afterward. It was a clear violation of his contract, especially when others came forward about him and his unwarranted actions against them. We're better off without him."

"Wow." Piper leans back into her own seat. "I never liked him."

"Really?" That's news to me.

"Why not?" Cassie asks.

"He treated me like I was beneath him. Like I had no right to be in my position doing what I do."

"I guess we're taking out all the trash in one go," Cassie says with a sigh. "He treated me like I was an idiot too."

"Why did we keep him around? I mean, he was a decent coach, but kind of a dick."

Coach Barney runs the show around here. Coach Cooper on the other hand? Well, he liked to flex his power by making us run the worst drills.

Good riddance as far as I'm concerned.

"Now, for real, get out of here." Cassie stalks around her desk and opens her office door. "Stay on my good side, Williams."

"You got it." I wink at her as I follow Piper out of the office.

Piper needs to get to the physio room, and I need to hit the weight room for a light workout before our game tonight.

But after hearing the news, I need a minute with my girl.

With my Princess.

"Where are we going?"

I lead Piper down a hallway, opening a few doors until I find a supply closet that is blissfully empty.

"I can't believe they're gone." I hoist Piper in my arms and push her against the wall. "We don't have to worry about them anymore."

Tears well in Piper's eyes. "I never thought I'd be so glad to see someone be cut."

I pepper her face in kisses. "Same, Princess. Same."

Piper grabs my face in her hands and kisses me hard. She flicks her tongue into my mouth.

We fight for control. The push and pull with Piper is something I love. Something that I will never have to let go of.

Piper is squirming in my arms, arching into my touch. It has my cock growing hard.

I rip my lips from hers. "Fuck, Piper. We can't do this right now."

"I want you, Cash," she whines.

"Princess, we can't," I say, even as I rock my hips into her. "I'll see you tonight after the game."

"At home."

I growl, nipping at her jaw. "You'll be waiting in my bed for me?"

"You better play nice with the reporters, Cash Williams. I'd hate to have to use my vibrator before you get there."

"God damn it, Piper. How am I supposed to get a workout with a hard-on?"

Piper wiggles in my arms, sliding down my body and standing on her feet.

"Something you'll need to figure out."

A smug smile is on her face as she turns to open the door.

"That's just mean."

I tug her back against me, pushing my hard cock against her sweet little ass.

"You better be ready, Princess. I'm going to ravish you tonight."

"Sounds like a plan."

"One minute left!" someone yells down the bench.

One minute left and the Colorado Black Diamonds are Stanley Cup Champions. We're up 4-2 against Detroit, and our guys are out there skating hard.

The home crowd is cheering loud, knowing the win is within our grasp. It's been a hard-fought playoff run to get here. No game is a given. We had to play the full seven games in a few series, but now? Now it's game five and we're getting ready to take this thing home.

In front of our home crowd.

Detroit's goalie is pulled, giving them an extra man, but it doesn't help. The seconds are ticking away. Long seconds that seem like they are stretching on for hours.

Troy shoots the puck down the ice, just missing the empty goal. Detroit is flying down the ice and grabs the puck, but it's useless.

"Three, two, one!"

The fans explode as all of us leap over the bench.

"Your Colorado Black Diamonds are Stanley Cup

Champions!" The announcer's voice booms over the loud speaker.

"Holy shit!"

Gloves are flying as the guys all pile down on top of Nick at the other end of the ice. I have no idea who I'm hugging as we all clamor together. Fans are banging on the glass in front of us.

It's the best feeling in the world as we line up to shake hands with the players from Detroit. Their heads hang as we make our way down the line.

That's a feeling I never want to experience. Losing the biggest game of your life while having to shake hands with the winning team. They skate off the ice, not wanting to hang around a minute longer than they have to.

"That was a pretty good goal you had there," Noah tells me, slinging his arm around my shoulders. "Don't think we would've pulled ahead without it."

"Nah," I brush him off. "We would've gotten it."

There's no way we would've lost this game at home. The energy tonight was something I've never felt before. Even during our first Stanley Cup run.

That one was about as easy as it gets.

This season, we had to fight. Fight for every goal and every win. Nothing about it came easy.

It makes it that much sweeter that we'll get to lift the cup over our heads.

Carpets are being rolled out for reporters and members of the Black Diamonds' staff to come out onto the ice.

Bexley Hart, the team owner's daughter, is congratulating everyone around her. With her taking over more of team operations this season, I have no doubt it's just as sweet for her.

On-ice reporters are already making their way to us.

There's hardly a moment to breathe as a Stanley Cup Championship hat is placed on my head.

"Think you have some time for a reporter?" Cassie asks, sauntering up to me.

"Come to gloat?"

"Who, me? Never." A playful smile is on her face.

"For you, Cassie? Always. You won't even have to tell me what to say."

"About damn time, Willy."

Cassie gives me a quick hug before a mic gets shoved in my face.

"Cash, how does it feel to win the cup?"

My eyes find Piper's as the families are waiting to come onto the ice after the trophy is presented. I think of her. Of the season the two of us have had together. Of the love we share and still get to share.

"Fucking incredible."

The reporter winces.

"Sorry. But I don't know if anything can match this feeling. Our team fought hard throughout the playoffs, and for all that work to pay off feels amazing."

"Your second Stanley Cup win with the Black Diamonds. How is this one different from the last?"

Not a single person has left the arena — not even Detroit fans. The Cup hasn't come out yet, but everyone wants a glimpse of the greatest trophy in sports.

At least in my opinion.

"It's different because I get to celebrate this win with my girlfriend."

The reporter's eyes go wide. "I think that's the most I've ever heard you talk about your personal life."

I laugh because I know it's true. "I guess Piper is a good influence on me."

"Well, go celebrate the win with her and your team. Thanks, Cash."

"Thank you."

Guys are ecstatic. Some of them are wiping tears from their eyes and others are taking in the crowd.

Only a few of them were here when we won last time.

For most, this is the first time winning the cup.

"I can't believe this." Troy wraps an arm around my shoulders.

"It might take a while to sink in."

Time seems to slow down and speed up all in the same breath. The cup is presented to the team and Bexley gives a speech about the team this year. It's hard to hear over the crowd's excitement. I'm bursting to lift that trophy up. To finally haul Piper into my arms and lay one on her.

Bexley stands by the cup before it's given to the coach and then passed off to Troy, who does his victory lap.

Surreal.

It's the only way to describe how I'm feeling right now as the cup eventually makes its way toward me.

I take it and start my lap around the ice. It feels weightless in my hands as I lift it over my head. Skating toward where the families are waiting behind the glass, I easily spot Piper.

She cups her hands around her mouth and cheers as I skate in front of her. "Lookin' good, Cash Williams!"

I shoot a wink her way as I pass off the cup to Noah.

"Yeah, baby!" He takes the cup, cheering as he skates off with it.

When I won my first cup with Colorado, I was a baby of a player. Now that I'm more seasoned, this win feels different.

Maybe it's because I feel closer to these guys than I ever have in the past. Maybe it's because I'm older and I can appreciate that I won't get to do this for the rest of my life.

Or maybe it's all because of Piper and getting to celebrate this win with her tonight. I look over to where she is, and her eyes are locked on me.

Finally, after what feels like forever, the families come onto the ice. Piper's parents head toward Noah, but Piper does her best to walk over to me.

"You won!" I catch her before she falls and haul her into my arms. "I can't believe it."

Her face is wet with tears as she peppers my face with kisses.

"Did you doubt us?" I hold her close to me.

She's already got a championship hat on. Happiness is radiating out from her.

"You know how nervous I get!" Piper flips my own hat around on my head so she can lay a kiss on my lips. "I couldn't sit still."

"I can't imagine being nervous at all."

She swats at me. "Cash!"

I press a kiss to her neck. "I love you, Princess."

"I love you, my Stanley Cup Champion."

My heart feels like it could burst out of my chest. I don't ever remember feeling this happy before. Even the last win doesn't hold a candle to this.

Because getting to hold Piper in my arms is about the best damn thing in the world.

"You know, I was a champion before."

Piper drops her forehead to mine, wrapping her arms around my neck. "That doesn't count. I wasn't dating you then."

"Dating doesn't feel like the right word," I tell her.

"Are we going to have this discussion now?"

I shrug a shoulder. "I've got nothing else to do right this very second."

"What am I going to do with you?" Piper shakes her head, laughing at me.

She's beaming, tears still wet on her face. With her jersey and championship hat on, she is the most beautiful person in the world.

"I have a few thoughts…"

"Oh yeah?" Her eyes are sparkling.

I nod, kissing her again before setting her on her feet. "None that would be appropriate to tell you here."

The crowd is starting to thin out as the guys make their way to the locker room. Champagne will be popped. Beers will be downed. And that's all before we head out to a club that will be reserved just for us and our families tonight.

"Well then, let's get these celebrations underway. I want to hear all about them." Piper shoves me away. "Now go celebrate so we can celebrate together later."

I give her one last kiss on the ice, wanting to commit everything about this moment to memory.

The win.

The cup.

The love of my damn life.

It all comes back to her.

Piper.

I never thought when Cassie set the two of us up that we would be here. Falling in love and joining our lives together.

Me and her. It's the only thing that does matter.

And I will spend every minute of my life making sure she knows.

Was Piper in the plans?

No.

But you know what they say about the best laid plans…

Bonus Epilogue

"I could get used to this."

"You know we leave tomorrow."

"Don't remind me, Cash."

I sit up, wiggling my toes into the sand. The sun is baking my skin. Waves lap up over the beach as the tide comes in. It's our own quiet haven here. Not a soul is around us.

Cash rented a villa for us, complete with its own private beach.

Palm trees hide the open air villa behind us. If we haven't been here, we've been at the pool. And every night, we spend our time on the patio, watching the sunset while eating the most delicious meals Cash has cooked up.

To say it's been perfect is an understatement.

"Need more time here?"

Sitting up, Cash kisses my shoulder where my new tattoo is. The one that matches the one over his heart.

The amaryllis flower.

"Not ready to go back to the real world."

After the Stanley Cup win, Cash surprised me with a

trip to Hawaii. Between graduation and playoffs, the two of us haven't had much time alone. Two uninterrupted weeks together?

It's been heaven.

"C'mon." Cash pops up, grabbing my hand. "Let's go cool off."

His flexing muscles distract me. I don't know if I'll ever get over how sexy he is, this man that I'll soon get to come home to every night.

"You're taking too long."

It's the only warning I get before Cash lifts me up and over his shoulder and runs toward the water.

"Cash!" I shriek.

He crashes into the water, which splashes up and over both of us. Cash makes like he's going to drop me, but pulls me into his arms instead.

"That was just mean!" I'm laughing as I lock my ankles around his hips.

"I would never drop you, Princess."

Cash drags a finger down my nose.

"You better not."

He squeezes me closer. The feel of him against me has heat gathering in my core. *Will this feeling ever go away?*

"I like you right here. Where you belong."

"Yours," I confirm. "Always yours, Cash."

He drags a hand down my back, playing with the ties of my bikini top.

"Mine." It's a growl as he steals a kiss. Swallowing my gasp, his tongue tangles with mine.

I sink into his touch, clawing at him to keep him close. He tastes like salt and rum from our drinks. It's a heady sensation.

"Cash," I moan.

He nips at my lips. The smile on his lips is sinful. It's the one that turns me to mush.

"Distracted?"

"You always distract me," I tell him.

"Like it's been easy for me to lie on the beach next to you?"

He grinds into me. The feel of his hard cock does things to my insides that I want to take full advantage of.

"Mmm. Is this something I can help you with?"

My hand drifts down his chest, toying with the waistband on his swim shorts.

"You better not start anything that you can't finish, Princess."

I push the material down. "I'll always finish everything I start with you."

"God damn it."

Cash leans over, sucking on the tender skin of my breast. He drags the material down with his teeth, exposing my hard nipple.

"I love that I turn you on like this."

"Always." I'm breathless.

His mouth drives me crazy. Each pass of his tongue has me dragging my hand up and down his pierced length.

"I need to be inside you."

"Do it."

Cash slips a hand between us, pushing the skimpy material to the side so he can slide inside of me.

"Gah!" I throw my head back in pleasure as he undoes my top.

It drifts to the shore with the waves as he swivels his hips, hitting that spot only he knows how to. Cash's moves are unhurried. My fingers dig into his back, wanting to pull him in as close as possible.

It's been like this all week.

Lying on the beach, sipping on rum cocktails. Playing in the water. Lazy make-out sessions followed by the best sex of my life.

It's been the perfect vacation.

All because of the man that is showering me with so much love and attention, I don't know what I did to deserve it.

"Cash!"

Cash holds me close as he continues to pump his hips inside me. It doesn't take much before he's exploding inside of me.

The only thing I can hear is the rush of the water in my ears as Cash laves my neck and chest with kisses.

"Piper."

Cash slips out of me, discarding the rest of our suits. If it weren't for his arms holding me to him, I'd float away in a state of pure bliss.

He walks us toward the shore, dropping down into the surf with me between his legs.

"How does this compare?" I ask him, pulling his arms around me.

"Compare to what?"

"To winning the Stanley Cup."

My eyes are closed as the sun continues to warm us. We sink into the sand as the tide comes in around us.

"Doesn't compare at all."

"What?"

I turn to face him, resting my hands on his thighs.

"Don't you get it?" He tucks a wet strand of hair behind my ear. "Nothing will ever compare to being with you, Piper. You're it for me."

"How did I get so lucky?"

Cash shakes his head, pulling me into him. My naked

chest brushes against his as he leans back. "I'm the lucky one."

"I love you."

Emotions are bubbling over, tears gathering in my eyes.

This wasn't supposed to be a thing. A means to an end for Cash to improve his reputation. I never thought it would turn into this.

Into a love that has grown into something I never expected. The biggest, most beautiful thing in my life.

"Hey, why the tears?" Cash wipes a stray tear away.

"Can't I just be happy because I love you?"

"Princess,"—he presses a kiss to my sun-warmed skin —"I don't think I've ever been happier in my life."

"Even when I move in?"

He nods, dragging his nose along my jaw. "Even happier when you move in and I get to see you every day."

I've been spending every night at Cash's. There's no point for me to have my own place anymore. As soon as we get back, we're moving me into his place.

Just the three of us.

"I can't wait."

I know it won't be easy. I'll be looking for a new job soon, and Cash will be returning to training in a few weeks. But there's no one else I want to take on this life with other than Cash.

Because he was the plan I never expected to make.

Our life will be crazy. But the one thing I can always plan on?

Cash Williams will be by my side.

Through thick and thin. Through everything.

And I wouldn't have it any other way.

Author's Note

BOOK NUMBER EIGHTEEN IS OUT IN THE WORLD!

It's hard to believe book two in the Black Diamonds is already out! Cash and Piper's story has been so loud in my head, and it was so easy to write. Cash is delightfully grumpy, and Piper is the perfect sunshiney woman for him! Add in little Puck, and I love this little family of mine!

There are so many people I want to thank. Kelly Reynolds for sprinting with me and getting this book done! To Menorah and Trish for beta reading and being on this journey with me. To all my incredible author friends, who are too many to name here. You know I love you!

To my Street Team and the Silver Society…I love getting to share my books with you and your excitement for them. Thank you to all the readers everywhere…for sharing and loving on my books and characters! There aren't enough words to thank you for your support!

<3 Emily

Also by Emily Silver

Colorado Black Diamonds Hockey

Best Kept Secret

Best Laid Plans

Best of the Best - coming July 31

Best of Both Worlds - coming October 31

Nashville Knights

Game Misconduct - Marcus and Harper's story, coming February 2025

Dixon Creek Ranch

Yours to Take

Yours to Hold

Yours to Be

Yours to Forget

Yours To Lose

Yours To Love - a newsletter freebie

The Denver Mountain Lions

Roughing The Kicker

Pass Interference

Sideline Infraction

Illegal Contact

The Big Game

Standalones

Off the Deep End — a MM sports romance

The Highland Escape - coming August 15

Merry in Moose Falls - coming November 21

The Ainsworth Royals

Royal Reckoning

Reckless Royal

Royal Relations

Royal Roots

The Love Abroad Series

An Icy Infatuation

A French Fling

A Sydney Surprise

Get the trope guide on my website, or
scan the QR code to read my books now!

About the Author

After winning a Young Author's Award in second grade, Emily Silver was destined to be a writer. She loves writing inclusive stories, with strong heroines and the swoony men who fall for them.

A lover of all things romance, Emily started writing books set in her favorite places around the world. As an avid traveler, she's been to all seven continents and sailed around the globe.

When she's not writing, Emily can be found sipping cocktails on her porch, reading all the romance she can get her hands on and planning her next big adventure!

Find her on social media to stay up to date on all her adventures and upcoming releases!